Run Wild

CALEB RAND

A Black Horse Western

ROBERT HALE · LONDON

© Caleb Rand 2000
First published in Great Britain 2000

ISBN 0 7090 6776 3

Robert Hale Limited
Clerkenwell House
Clerkenwell Green
London EC1R 0HT

Typeset by
Derek Doyle & Associates, Liverpool
Printed and bound in Great Britain by
Antony Rowe Limited, Wiltshire

Run Wild

1
The Ambush

Ethan gently led the black gelding across the low, eastern slopes of the mountain ridge. He whispered encouragement as the horse snickered and trembled its way through the scree. For the first part of his journey to Santa Rosa, he'd ridden more than 150 miles to cross the peaks of the Sangre de Christos.

The dense, metallic sky crushed down. The summer sun rose higher as an immense brazen disc. It singed Ethan's skin, seared his lungs, and he pinched his neck-cloth up close around his face. Sweat ran into the crimps of his skin, the bridle-reins were constantly slipping through the soapy wetness of his hands and his bright-blue eyes stung from salt.

Ethan dismounted at a sloping bank of the Pecos River and grinned at the violent snorting of his horse. It was startled at the sudden bite of water around its warm nostrils; then alarmed, as the crack of a rifle-shot cut the still, heat-laden air.

Ethan felt the sharp pulse of the bullet as it passed his right temple. He swore as in one swift movement he grabbed his .52 Spencer and rolled down and away from his saddle. He landed painfully on his left shoulder, violently twisting his body into the scrubby grass. Lying on his back, he levered a shell into the breech of the carbine.

He was assessing the scrub for cover when the next bullet took the frightened gelding high on its forehead. He watched, breathless and spellbound as the horse convulsed. It stomped a pace forward, before buckling heavily to the ground. Still clutching the rifle, Ethan managed a half-crouch, then he lunged. With his free hand, he clasped the soft, blood-covered muzzle for the few seconds it took his stricken horse to die.

Ethan ground his teeth in anguish, then raised his head. He glared east, back at the stunted pine he'd ridden through earlier. He fired, waited for the echo of the shot to slam into the side of the foothills, then pumped six more bullets into the rock-strewn outcrop. He rolled on to his back, squeezed his eyes shut, and with the rifle clutched tight across his chest, silently counted the seconds. After ten, he ran, fast at a crouch. He zigzagged back up the scree, trusting in his retaliation to give him time.

Ethen made the outcrop, and went into a crawl. He edged through the scree, alert for the slightest movement ahead of him. He saw the pine and rock he'd blasted, listened to the crushing silence. He stood up slowly and took a few cautious paces. Then he saw the ambusher, spread and unmoving in the blistered scree. He was a lean man, hatless, wearing the worn colourless clothes of a drifter. A single-shot, Sharps rifle lay near his outstretched arm. There was a plug-mule standing off, hobbled and fractious.

Ethan walked to the man's side and poked him with the tip of his carbine. There was a feeble groan, and the man twisted his head. His eyes were clouded, and a trickle of gummy blood oozed close to Ethan's skin boots.

Ethan hunkered down and spoke quick and sharp. 'Looks like your inside's been shot through, mister, an' there's nothin' I can do. But tell me why you shot the horse and I'll make your dyin' easier.'

The man gurgled and spat, his words faltering and hardly audible. 'Not the horse . . . you.' He raised his doom-filled eyes to Ethan. 'Reckon yer not him . . . Goddammit . . . looked like you . . . from a distance.'

The man's jaw sagged, and his face fell against the rough, hard ground. Ethan kneeled, and he bent close.

'Who? Who looks like me? Who'd you think I was? You killed my horse, you sumbitch. Tell me. You owe me that,' he shouted at the gunman.

'Wheat . . . Calum Wheat . . . I was told that . . . features an' all. . . .' The man's eyes cramped, and his breath hissed and rasped.

Ethan eased himself up. He pulled at his bandanna, smearing a film of sweat and sand across his face, looked thoughtfully out across the blistering range. His gelding was dead, and he'd no intention of making the man's dying any easier.

He thought of the message he carried in his pocket, and despite the overpowering heat, a shiver rippled through his body. Calum Wheat was his younger brother.

2
Rancher's Feud

After a short easement and retying of his traps, Ethan urged the mule down to the grassland near the scorched-earth borders, west of the llano. He loosed the reins, gripped firmly with his legs and once again read the short note he'd received in Durango, Colorado. It was from Calum, and read: COME HOME. RANCH IN TROUBLE, BRING A GUN.

There weren't many words, but already Ethan had been touched by the fact. A man had just died, and he'd to wonder on the cause of it. A family feud? An armed dispute over land- or water-rights?

Making Santa Rosa, then S River Ranch before nightfall, was out of the question with the crossbreed mount and Ethan patiently rode east. After nearly three hours, beside a low run of the Rio Chama, he stopped beneath the shadows of some live-oaks. He handed the mule a few pieces of dried fruit, then, removing his Bowie knife, stretched himself fully dressed in the fast-running water. After a few minutes he rolled on to his front, raised himself on to his elbows. He looked up and saw the mule flicking its ears worriedly. He stumbled to his knees, slipping and sliding on the stony river bed. He sloshed through the shallows to the bank and looked across the flat grassland. Against the soft murmur of the water-race, all he heard was the drip of water from his long, buckskin jacket. Then he heard the alien sound that he knew was all wrong; it was the noise of a rope as it cut the still air. The mule was aware of it first. It whinnied, then jerked away as a loop fell around Ethan's neck and arms. Ethan made an instinctive move for his rifle, but it was tied into the saddle traps. He was pulled a step backward before stumbling to the ground.

From behind one of the nearby oaks, a man stepped forward, then two more followed. The first man advanced on the mule; he jumped at its bridle, but backed off when the animal baulked, lashed out with its front feet. The other two men flung themselves at Ethan and held him to the ground.

He'd been caught, and in flaring anger and retaliation Ethan drove his right foot fearfully into a man's face. He heard the man yell, and immediately he lunged upward to head-butt the second attacker. He'd rolled away, and was just getting to his knees when the frame of a hand-gun slammed into the side of his head.

'Put him down, Moss,' was all he heard. There was no pain, just a silver flash, and the early evening light changed to blackness.

*

Ethan stirred, then groaned. He was slumped in the saddle of the mule, and a rope hung crudely around his neck. He opened his eyes, and a grim, bearded face loomed up beneath him. The man called Moss said, 'You're ridin' a Big Log mule, Mister. Where'd you get it?'

Ethan tried to raise his hands, but they were tied tight behind his back. He opened his mouth to speak, and the pain tore into his head. 'I took it from someone who tried to kill me. But he shot my horse.'

A small man with a split lip and a crushed, bloodied nose pushed in. 'Looks like mule-stealin' to me,' he snarled, thickly. 'That's what we'll be hangin' you for.'

Ethan tried to shake off the sting of pain. 'I told you. I didn't steal the mule.'

Moss spat into the ground at the mule's feet. 'That's what they all say, mister. But that mule's from the Big Log spread, an' so are we.'

Ethan twisted in the saddle. He sensed that telling the whole truth wouldn't improve the situation. He looked at the noose. It was tied to the branch of oak above his head. 'I guess you ain't figgurin' on a trial?'

'Not in Barton Ringwood's garden,' Moss railed. 'Horse-thieves get strung up as soon as we catch 'em, an' that mule's near enough for me.'

Ethan glared defiantly at the men around him. He'd seen a hanging once, along the Dolores, east of Durango. He could still see the thin, stretched body jerking at the end of a knotted rope; tattered boots snapping out a jig. Twenty terrifying seconds of a dying man's last dance, and crude smirks for the inept hangman. Ethan felt his insides run cold, shivered, as he strained at his bound wrists.

Calum Wheat licked a short pencil-stub, then wrote a number for the last of the Texas longhorns. For a few seconds, he looked pensively at the S River tally.

He shouted out at his foreman, Budge Gourley. 'Yeah, looks like you're right, Budge. There's another couple a dozen missin'. That's close on a hundred we've lost since late June.' Calum's eyes swept across his dwindling herd. 'At this rate we're gonna be cleaned out before winter sets in.'

'I know'd it, Cal.' Budge looked unhappily at his boss. He took off his beaten-up Stetson and scratched his head. 'If yer gonna believe they're just wanderin' out the end of the valley, then I'm a Holy Moses. We'd a seen 'em and we ain't, none of us have, not even the nighthawks. They're still disappearin', an' it sure beats the hell outa me.'

Calum rolled the scrap of tally paper around the pencil and pushed it into his vest pocket. He uncurled his leg from around the horn of his saddle. 'It's the damn llano. You can run off the cattle, an' take 'em out a few miles. You can lose yourself out there, an' anyone else who's following. Run a herd east, all the way to Texas, an' no one'll ever know.'

Budge slammed his hat back on to his head and pulled the brim down sharply. 'Well, who do you think's behind it? It'd help if we knew, give us a start, like.'

'It's Barton Ringwood. Who the hell else could it be,

Budge?' Calum was of a mild, unruffled nature, but now his voice carried the bite of ill-temper.

Budge nodded consideringly. 'What's he after? The cattle or the land?'

'More than that, Budge. He wants everything. Every damn thing he sees.'

'How's he gonna get S River?'

'He wants Festus to marry Marge.'

Budge spluttered a gob of tobacco juice. 'Doggone it, Cal, owls throw up healthier lookin' stuff than Festus Ringwood.'

'Yeah, I know, but getting Festus into the family makes it easy an' legal. The boy's already tried it on, but I sent him packin'. He didn't like it, an' his old man liked it less. The Ringwoods don't take kindly to bein' told no. They get what they want out here. If they don't, then they'll turn nasty, look to harm you. That's what they're doin', Budge.'

Budge stared around him. 'How about we move the herd into the brakes? There's water, an' we could kinda lose 'em in the bracken. It's high enough.'

Calum lashed out at a rising cloud of midges. 'Oh, we'd lose 'em well enough, an' at this time a year there's not enough water to hold a newt. You know that for Chris'sakes, Budge. Can't you come up with anything better than that.'

Two of Calum's cowhands who'd moved in to listen to the conversation looked at each other uneasily, then turned their horses back in the direction of the ranch. Calum watched the men move away, then held the palms of his hands towards Budge. He made a grim smile.

'Sorry, Budge. I was expectin' you to talk shotgun. Wantin' to take down a few walls.'

'Yeah, well, failin' that, what else you got in mind?'

'I've sent for help. There's someone in Arizona might back us up.'

'You've written to Ethan?'

'Yeah. Sent a message to Durango. Told him to bring a gun. If he's comin' he can't be far away now.' Calum gave a 'move-off' command to his pony and flicked the reins. 'We'll follow Ralph and Starling back. We can't do much out here.'

Calum rode in dejected silence. He was considering the hostility between himself and the Big Log owner. Long gone were the days when neighbouring families shared their land trails.

Since his last run-in with young Festus Ringwood, Calum had contended with rustled cattle and burned-out line-shacks. But more recently there were other ways in which Barton Ringwood was vexing him. The powerful rancher had a 'mooch' in the Youngsville law office: the ineffectual alcoholic, Chew Heddon. Heddon was regularly jailing S River punchers for so-called 'hell raising', whereas he conveniently overlooked any real trouble from the Big Log crew. Never much, but calculated to disturb and chafe at Calum.

The Wheat brothers' sister, Marge, hadn't escaped the rub of Barton Ringwood's malice either. Calum had caught Festus pestering her on her return from a provision run to Youngsville. The young braggart's mouth had run away with him, and in front of Marge, Calum was forced to smack him around a bit before packing him off to Big Log. That turned into scuttle-butt about there being more than one brood mare out at S River. But Ringwood hadn't fully thought out the crude slur against Marge. He was shooting himself and his son in the foot with that one.

Calum squinted into the distance. Budge was riding close behind, but Ralph and Starling had disappeared into the range. Calum knew the time had come for some sort of retaliation, but he had to wait for his brother to return to S River; wait for the obliging gun.

Before he could get far with his thoughts, Calum's attention switched to the horizon. Against the dipping sun, he could see a rider heading furiously towards them. Budge edged in, and they watched for a full minute as the rider drew near.

Nate Starling rushed his horse between the two men. He was breathless and excited as he reined in his sweating mount. 'Up ahead . . . west a bit . . . about a mile. We were takin' the horses for a drink . . . under the oak stand . . . they're gonna lynch someone.' He faltered, and Calum made a grab for the horse's bridle.

'Who? Who's lynchin' who?'

'Big Log riders . . . that new ramrod . . . Moss . . . he's there. Dunno who they're stringin' up . . . back was to us. There ain't no doubt though . . . saw the rope.'

It was gut instinct that drove Calum's spurs deep into his cow-pony's flanks.

3

The Wheat Brothers

It was the simultaneous set of four rifle hammers that stopped the hanging.

Ethan Wheat heard the sounds in his head, tried to make sense of it. He hadn't closed his eyes, but they were unseeing in the dark world he was making ready for.

He got the voice as it sliced through the oak stand.

'If that mule so much as whickers its nose, Moss, you'll all die before my brother does.'

Ethan turned his head, his jawbone wedging against the crude hangman's-knot. He looked into the eyes of Calum who was less than thirty feet away. He was kneeling atop a low ridge bankside to the Chama.

Ethan's stomach churned as he fought the rising sickness. He stared at Moss who was going to whack the mule with the barrel of his rifle.

'Careful, goat-face,' he rasped. 'My brother never was much good with a rifle. He'll more than likely take ten shots before you die.'

Calum and Starling walked slowly down to the group of men standing around Ethan's mule. Budge and Ralph covered them, while Calum cut the string around Ethan's wrists. Ethan reached up and inched the noose from around his neck, his eyes boring into Moss as he climbed from his saddle. He reached for the rifle in the man's hands and wrenched it from him.

'Now, as I was tellin' you,' he said flatly. 'I never stole that mule. My name's Ethan Wheat, and if you don't know already, that there's my brother Calum.' He took a step back and smiled grimly. 'Those with good memories would say I'm the hot-tempered one. Can't think why.'

With that, he swung the barrel with muscle and anger. The yard of steel poled into the front of Moss's bearded face, and the assembled men winced at the terrifying noise of breaking bone.

Ethan looked closely at the rifle, then tossed it to the man he'd head-butted half an hour earlier. 'Take it,' he said, 'nothin's broken.'

As Budge and Ralph approached from the ridge, the man turned to Calum as if for support. 'No one knew it was your brother, Wheat. You know what happens out here . . . when . . . we. . . .'

The man's words trailed away when he saw Ethan step menacingly towards him. But Ethan simply eyeballed each of the men as he removed their guns and belts.

Calum shook his head vigorously. 'You ain't hangin' any man in this county, mister. Put together your ramrod's head and ride away. Don't bother to come back for your guns, but if you stay in Santa Rosa, give a message to Barton Ringwood. Tell him from now on he'll be dealin' with *two* Wheats.'

Ralph and Starling watched as Ringwood's men heaved Moss across his saddle. One of the men turned to Calum.

'Mr Ringwood ain't gonna like this. No sir, you're scratchin' him the wrong way.'

Calum pulled Ethan's traps and led the mule over to the man. He handed him the reins. 'Just tell Mr Ringwood to stay away from S River,' was all he said.

Then, spitting, pulling faces and muttering half-hearted insults. the men climbed on to their own horses and rode south in the direction of Big Log.

A minute later Ethan and Calum were making a tentative, cool reunion. Ethan touched the weal on the side of his neck. 'You should have sent a fuller message, brother. There's some of it you missed out.'

Calum smiled. 'Couldn't spell *lynching*,' he said. He looked his brother up and down, noticed there was no hand-gun. 'You ain't carryin' Pa's old hog-leg,' he remarked.

'I've still got it.' Ethan pointed at his traps. 'You just said to bring it, remember?' Then he nodded amicably as Calum introduced him to Starling and Ralph.

Budge grinned big and held out his hand. 'You can ride with me, Ethan,' he said. 'It's been a time. Good to see you again.'

In the first dark, as the S River men rode back to the ranch, Ethan shouted across at Calum. 'How's our little sister? She still buildin' them apple-pies?'

'Marge ain't so little any more, Ethan.' Calum's eyes flicked to Budge. 'Ain't that so, Budge?'

4

Ringwood's Dream

Big Log ranch was sheltered in the darkness. There was a crescent of yucca and blackgum; a sturdy dogwood draped its thick branches across the ranch house.

Barton Ringwood sat in his study, fingers drumming irritably on the edge of his desk. 'Where's Moss, now?' he asked the man standing in front of him.

'In the bunkhouse. His head's busted up real bad, Mr Ringwood. He won't be sayin' much for a while.'

Ringwood smirked. 'Looks like he got to you too, Ketchum.'

'He's no greenhorn. We never know'd Wheat had a brother, Mr Ringwood. He's a mean son of a bitch, an' that's a fact. Said someone shot his horse. I guess he coulda been tellin' the truth.'

'What makes you say that?'

'The mule,' Ketchum said. 'It belonged to Charlie Lemon. You fired him last week. He wouldn't have got far on that piece a crowbait you gave him.'

'But he shot the horse Wheat was ridin', you fool.'

'He was a cheap, no-good drifter, Mr Ringwood. You said so yourself. I guess he missed.'

Ringwood didn't respond at once. For a few seconds he chewed his lip, lost in prospect. 'So, Ethan Wheat's come home, has he?' he mumbled to himself. Then he raised his head, and snapped, 'There's gonna be some changes round here, Ketchum. Calum Wheat's not the only one who thought of gettin' himself a gun. Now get out, and tell Pelt to come see me.'

As Ketchum sloped from the room, Ringwood shouted after him, 'And send someone into town for Heddon.'

Ringwood eased himself back from his desk. He opened a deep drawer and pulled out a bottle of Kentucky bourbon. He poured two fat fingers, and considered taking it down in one. It was true that he'd fired Charlie Lemon, and the mule was a shrewd touch. But he'd also paid the man two months' wages to put a bullet into Calum Wheat.

Barton Ringwood was desperate for S River ranch. From a loose-tongued surveyor, he'd learned that within two years the Butterfield stage route would be overtaken by the Southern Pacific Railroad.

Reaching El Paso had once meant Big Log herds freely crossing the southern limits of S River land, with its good water and graze. But since the outbreak of hostilities, the alternative route was a long loop east, then down through the Loving Salt Flats. A journey ill-suited to the schemes of Barton Ringwood.

He'd already approached the railroad owners about the possibility of a 'named' cattle stop. When that happened, the ambitious rancher would create his dream; a mighty cattle trade from Los Angeles in the west, eastward to New Orleans.

Shortly before his death, Dempster Wheat had willed his real estate to his daughter, Marge. To the old man's reckoning, he'd made his own way in life, and his boys could do the same. Calum stayed on, working with his sister, but it was no secret that it drove Ethan out of Santa Rosa. To Barton Ringwood, his return was bad news, and it rattled him.

Ringwood was pouring another drink when the door suddenly opened. A slim-built man stood calmly in the doorway. He wore a short, dark waistcoat, colour-matched boots and hat. Mallen Pelt was a mercenary gunman, and the rig of his trade was belted high.

Ringwood indicated that Pelt should take a seat. He put the bourbon bottle back in his desk drawer, pushed the glass towards the gunman.

'Seems like I picked the wrong man for a job, Pelt. It was the job you shoulda done, if you'd got here sooner.' Ringwood looked suitably impatient. 'Now there's two of 'em.'

The set of Pelt's face hardly moved from mild inter-est. 'Well that'll cost double what we agreed. Half now, the rest when it's done. I'll choose my own time.'

Ringwood nodded, weighing up the circumstances

as Pelt rolled his bourbon around the glass. 'As long as I'm payin' you Pelt, it's *my* time,' he said strongly. 'You take 'em in the open, in Youngsville. Mind how you set it up, and do it lawful. I don't want any US Marshal pokin' his nose in.'

Pelt placed his empty glass back on the desk. 'Any more advice for me, Mr Ringwood?'

'It ain't advice, Pelt,' Ringwood snapped. 'I thought that was how men like you stayed alive. Attention to detail. Using the advantage.'

Pelt sniffed, and Ringwood continued, 'The sheriff belongs to me. If you leave it late enough, he'll be too drunk to see. You shouldn't have any trouble with Calum Wheat. It'll be his brother, Ethan. From what I know of him, he's a hard one, wild an' looks it.'

Mallen Pelt just smirked thinly, as Ringwood pulled $250 from his billfold.

When the gunman had left the room, Ringwood slumped in his chair. He was still concerned, didn't want to be cozened by appearance.

It was late when Festus walked in on his father. Ringwood smiled tiredly as his only son raised a hand in silent greeting. Festus eyed the empty glass, then sat in the chair opposite. He was in his early twenties, medium height, but sturdy, after his father. He had a spurt of freckles across his nose, pale eyes and hair the colour of scrub. He was also a cowardly, self-indulgent layabout. His young life was filled with the bawdy spoils of Youngsville. Except for soliciting cash, talking to his father hardly ever figured.

'Taken over S River, yet?' he asked; a mix of mock and interest.

'Not yet,' his father sighed. 'I can't just move in. Had a bit of a set-back, but I'm workin' on it.'

'Workin' on it? It needs more'n that, Big Daddy,' Festus sneered.

Ringwood stared at his son. 'You remember Calum Wheat's brother, Ethan?'

'Yeah, I remember him. Rode off, years ago. Why?'

'He's come back, an' he's trouble. Makes things that more difficult.'

'For Chris'sake, you've got enough men and money to take care a him. He's only one. He ain't that good.'

'From what I've been told, he's too good for anyone around these parts.'

Festus leaned forward provocatively. 'That's what you've got the gunny here for. You'll be forkin' him a stack to take care of the Wheats.'

Ringwood shook his head slowly. 'You sure got a head on you, son. I suppose Mallen Pelt can sweeten things between you and the girl, Marge, eh? We have to play this out. Your tactics ain't got you far, Festus. You can't push.'

Festus glared at his father. 'That trouble I had was weeks ago. You told me you'd get it sorted.'

'I will. Be patient. You forgettin' the S River herd's dwindling? There'll be no more than scatterlin's before winter sets in. Moss's takin' care a that for me. Pelt'll do the same, you see. You'll get your pretty Miss Wheat. Maybe even as a wife.' Ringwood raised his eyebrows, worked a shallow grin.

Festus got to his feet. 'Well, thanks for the drink, Big Daddy, but I'm tellin' you, if it takes much longer, I'll be followin' Ethan Wheat's trail outa here.'

'Don't go squeezin' me, son. My appetite's just as great as yours, but all of a sudden we're playin' the longer game. Sometimes you have to sit awhile.'

After Festus had gone, Ringwood turned down the lamp, and walked through the quiet house. He sat on the stoop, listening to the crickets, looking at the stars over the peaks of the distant Sangre de Christos.

It was long after midnight when Chew Heddon rode in from Youngsville. The sheriff looped his horse to the hitching rail and stepped up to the ranch house. His voice carried its usual thickness. 'It's late, Barton. What do you want me for at this hour?'

'There's a horse-thief rode in from the north. I suspect he killed one a my men. You'll find him at S River. He'll be tough-lookin', and lean. Wears Indian. Find him and run him outa Santa Rosa. No need to make an arrest, I want him gone. You understand?'

Heddon held out his hands anxiously. 'I understand, Barton . . . Mr Ringwood. But if I knew his name?'

Ringwood stood up. 'Listen to me, Heddon. You ain't goin' out there to make friends. Just do the job, or you'll be drinking from the horse trough.'

Heddon wasn't going to argue. In Youngsville, he had a roof over his head and enough money for pine-top. Together with an occasional 'fruit' from the Red Dust saloon, life was just bearable. But the terms of office and his tenure were down to Barton Ringwood, and Heddon resented it.

As he rode back to town, the pushed-around sheriff considered his status. 'One day,' he muttered, 'one day, them Ringwoods'll pay.'

5

Reunion

In the fertile valley that separated the foothills of the Sangre de Christos from the llano, the Wheat's ranch house was snugged in one of two tight coils of the lower Pecos. There were outhouses, chicken-coops, a corral and a two-storey barn. The main house was small, but out of deference to the land, built thick and strong.

At the rear, straps of timber crossed a sharp, narrow curve of the river. Through stands of willow, tracks spread north; some rose west, up to the rock and wooded mountain foothills. From the front, where the winding course of the water nearly met it, a mile of wagon road led south from the ranch house before forking into the cattle trails around Youngsville. Beyond the S River grazing-land was El Paso, the Rio Grande and the Mexican border.

Apart from the yellow glow of lights from windows, the ranch was in deep darkness as the five riders approached.

Ethan was peering over Budge's shoulder. 'Do you

reckon Marge'll have us any supper, Budge?'

Budge answered back into the night. 'What's with the 'us' Ethan? It's late, an' she don't know you're comin' There'll be plenty for me an' Cal, but. . . .'

Ethan realized the truth behind Budge's humour, and for a moment felt uneasy, embarrassed about his return.

Leading the horses, Ralph and Starling went off to the bunkhouse. Calum and Budge clumped up the steps of the ranch house. Ethan was lagging behind. He'd gone back to pull something from his traps that Starling had been toting for him.

Calum knocked, called and stepped back, waiting for Marge to throw the crossbar. She stepped into the light that fell across the stoop. Calum and Budge moved aside, and she looked down at her elder brother.

Ethan pulled off his crumpled Stetson and, with one hand behind his back, bowed deeply.

Marge bit her lip, and when Ethan looked up he saw the glint that wetted her eyes.

'Hyah Marge,' he said, trying to sound as if he'd been out for a stomp around the yard or something.

'I knew Cal was up to something . . . but I never thought . . .' she said, faltering and soft.

'Got a present for you,' Ethan said, holding out his hand. 'Come an' get it.'

Marge shook her head. 'No, you come up here.'

Ethan grinned and moved up between Calum and Budge. 'Here. It's an Apache charm bag. Pretty, ain't it?'

As Ethan and Marge sparred with self-conscious remarks, Budge made his excuses. 'I'll be over in the

bunkhouse. There'll be things for you to . . . well, you
know.'

Calum winked at his discreet ramrod and ushered
his brother and sister into the house.

After eating, they talked until dawn. Ethan sprawled
in a comfortably stuffed chair and at his feet sat Elky,
the Tahl-Tan hunting-dog. Marge was sure it remembered it had been Ethan's pup, before he'd left for
Arizona. Marge eventually turned in. She left Calum
explaining the problem of Barton Ringwood and Big
Log ranch.

'He's set on getting hold of the ranch, Ethan. Takin''
over the valley's part of his campaign. It must be something big, but payin' for someone to kill me – you as it
turned out, that's serious stuff. Do you think he'll try
again?'

'If it's that important to him, yeah, reckon he will.
We'll need to watch our backs.' Ethan scratched the top
of Elky's head. 'How many men you got . . . we got?'

'Six, includin' Budge. Three less than we had a
couple a weeks ago. Can't afford to replace 'em.'

Ethan fixed his eyes on his brother. 'How's the
finances, then?'

'Not good. That's why we've got to make a drive to El
Paso. The mortgage is due.'

'Why not force Ringwood's hand? Overwinter the
herd. Make the drive, an' payment on the ranch, next
spring. Go speak to the bank manager about it.'

'His name's Gil Morrow, and I already have, Ethan.
He won't do it. He'll foreclose before Christmas.'

'Why?'

'Pressure from Ringwood. That's how he'll get the ranch, an' it's legal. He knows there's no future in Festus hitchin' up with Marge.'

Ethan shook his head in disbelief. 'I remember that kid. If his looks ain't matured any, we could run him outa Santa Rosa with the herd. Nobody'd take much notice of a runt yearling.'

Both men laughed, and the Tahl-Tan raised its head fractionally.

Ethan levered himself tiredly out of the chair. He walked to the window and Elky followed closely. He stared east, as the day's first silver skeins touched the distant mountains. 'I'll send for help, the same way you did, Cal. I know a couple of rebels who'll like the odds. No need to pay 'em, they owe me.'

Calum didn't say anything, just watched as the dog moved to sniff, then bark at the door.

Ethan looked at his brother. 'What's her problem, Cal?'

Calum was already reaching for a shotgun. 'Must be someone on the way in.'

Ethan walked over to his traps, and unrolled his big Navy Colt. He tucked it into his belt, then drew out the Spencer. 'Perhaps it starts now, Cal. Hope there's no more'n a dozen of 'em. I'm just too tired.'

Chew Heddon reined in his horse. He was flanked by two men who wore long, shabby dusters.

When Calum and Ethan appeared in the doorway the sheriff said something to his men.

'Speak up, Heddon. It's dark an' we don't want any mistakes,' Calum responded.

One of the men levered up a short-barrelled carbine. 'Do what you have to, Sheriff. They ain't gonna try anythin',' he grated.

'You've already made the mistake, Wheat.' Heddon smirked. 'That fella beside you, he's a horse-thief who's gonna leave the county.'

Calum shot a quick glance at his brother, then calmly waved his shotgun at the two deputies. 'The pine-top's got to you, Heddon. To my way of seein', you've only two men to back you up. You need a lot more'n that to throw your weight around on my property. There's no horse-thief here. You've rode a fair ways for nothin'.'

Ethan was eyeing all three men. As was Elky, crouched low and wary between his feet.

The deputy with the carbine made another movement and Ethan spoke up. 'These're no odds for you, mister. You'll be the one that dies. Do the sensible thing.'

The man threw a dark look at Heddon. 'We was never told it'd be like this. Set 'em on their way, you said.'

'You've drawn your last pay as a deputy, Burdett,' Heddon snarled. 'How 'bout you, Wallace?'

The other man wheeled his horse. 'I'm thinkin' Burdett's got a point,' he said. 'When I'm lookin' down the barrels of a big-bore, I don't see a horse-thief.'

'Get goin', Heddon, afore we set the dog on you,' Calum snorted.

'I'll get goin', Wheat. But the next time, I'll have me a warrant.'

'We'll be in town, soon enough,' Calum threatened.

Ethan stood bewildered as the lawmen took off into the darkness. He asked his brother. 'What's happenin'? What's the sheriff doin' out here?'

'It sure proves Ringwood's behind it all, but it's not as serious as you think, Ethan. Chew Heddon's a drunk, an' he's the sheriff, all right. But to him, the law plays second fiddle.'

'Not serious? What about that warrant he mentioned?'

'Forget it. There's nothin' to go on, and Judge Mallard plays it straight.'

Ethan turned and went back into the house, the dog followed closely. He stretched his arms and yawned. 'A few hours' sleep, brother, an' we'll ride into town together.'

'Apart from Heddon, anythin' particular in mind?' Calum asked.

'Have to send a wire to Durango. Get those boys down here, the ones I was tellin' you about. It'll take them a few days, and I can sure use the time.'

'What else you up to?'

Ethan was rubbing his eyes. 'I ain't doin' much until I've got me a horse, Cal. You know that.'

'Yeah, I guessed it. You always took to a fancy piece a horseflesh. There's nothin' good enough for you on the ranch.'

'Budge told me that this time a year there'll be a herd somewhere below the timberline. If they're there an' I see somethin', it shouldn't take more'n five days. I'll go after we've come back from Youngsville. And now if you don't mind, brother, I've had enough for one day.'

6

Meeting with a Gunman

In the Red Dust saloon one of a small group of colour-ful, perfumed ladies had been having a good look at Mallen Pelt. She flounced along the bar towards him. 'Hyah, fella,' she said.

She adjusted her shawl, and Pelt got an enticing glimpse of shoulder and shiny blue frills. She faked coyness when she saw him staring, but came directly to the point. 'I'm drinkin' if'n yer interested.'

Pelt answered casually. 'Could be.'

'Come on,' she said cheerily, and lightly brushed the man's fingers. 'Bella's as dry as the long, hot summer.'

Pelt grinned coldly, realizing the implication.

In a corner of the room two men were sitting close to a derelict pot-bellied stove. They were feet up, with their heels resting on a brass rail that ran circular around the top. They looked up doubtfully when Bella and her partner approached.

'Sorry, boys,' Bella said, 'but this tank's just come reserved.'

One of the men let his boots thump to the floor, but the other man got to his feet. 'Well I'm real sorry 'bout that,' he said, sarcastically. Then he caught the look in Pelt's eyes, and thought better of it. 'We'll find one that's not so *reeee*served.'

The first man looked down at the top of the stove. 'These are paid for,' he said. He picked up both glasses of whiskey in one hand, and drained them, together.

The barman walked over and banged a bottle and two short glasses in front of them. Bella smiled and reached for the bottle. She filled Pelt's glass, then her own. Impassively, the gunman watched her.

'Here's to men and women,' Bella said genially, and drained her glass.

'Some of 'em, ma'am.' As Pelt swallowed his own drink, his eyes swung searchingly around the saloon. He nodded at the bottle, and Bella reached out enthusiastically.

All four men had slept until noon. It was approaching first dark of the same day when they rode into Youngsville.

'Telegraph office in the same place, Calum?' Ethan asked, as they tied in to one of the main street's hitching rails.

'Yep. Take Budge with you. Me and Ralph'll meet you at the Prairie Dust.'

The brothers looked at each other. Concern sounded in Calum's voice 'If there's trouble, Ethan, that's where it'll find us. But we all need a drink.'

Slow and cautious, Ethan and Budge crossed the
street to the telegraph office. Elky, the bear-dog, shadowed close. Calum and Ralph moved along to the saloon.

The big bar was pungent and stifling, fogged with
the press of tobacco smoke. It was tail-end of the
month, when pay was drawn. Grangers and itinerant
cowboys from the ranches of Santa Rosa were drinking, playing chuckaluck and faro.

Every now and again Bella looked up. When Calum
and Ralph pushed through the swing doors, she whispered something to Pelt. The gunman tugged at the
front of his waistcoat, then at the cuffs of his cambric
shirt. He picked up his glass of whiskey and strode
leisurely to the end of the bar.

With his back to Pelt, Calum was talking to Ralph.
'Don't let me cramp your style, Ralph, if you see something you fancy. You know the way things are, but I can
give you ten dollars against future pay.'

Ralph looked around him. 'Right now, ten dollars is
a lot more'n I need, Calum. I'll go and talk about cattle
to Angie. She's interested in longhorns.'

Calum watched, laughed quietly, as Ralph's heaving
shoulders moved towards the colourful, perfumed
ladies. He moved his whiskey chaser to one side and
poured himself a glass of beer.

As he took his first long gulp of the frothed brew,
Mallen Pelt disturbed him.

'That smell of cows, you brought in with you, mister.
It's puttin' me off my drinkin'.

Calum went very still for a second, then shook his head. He put his beer on the counter, reached for the tumbler of whiskey. He turned slowly to Pelt. 'Well, ain't that a shame.' He looked the gunman up and down, noticed the high-fitted Colt. 'For me, I'm not sure it's enough to fight about, but for you . . . well, I guess maybe it is. I'll just move along the bar a ways.'

Calum felt the prospect of trouble. He looked at Pelt, and saw that a few steps away wouldn't be enough. He realized the gunman wanted him to create distance. Up close, sudden movement would be too concealed and confusing.

'Just ease off. I ain't lookin' for trouble,' Calum said. It wasn't what he wanted to say, but he'd never had his brother's ability with guns. He knew Pelt wouldn't shoot him in the back if he just walked away, but he couldn't do that.

Pelt knew it too, and he grinned viciously. 'You'll be lookin' for help, cowman if you carry on drinkin' while I'm talkin' to you.'

Calum saw Pelt's eyes flick to one side, and guessed, hoped that Ralph had made a move. 'There's two of us,' he said. 'Now that smell ain't half so bad, I'm bettin'.'

'Wrong,' Pelt, sneered. 'It's worse, an' it means another bullet.'

'Leave it, Calum,' Ralph shouted. 'He's only up to puttin' down broken cattle.'

Calum was never to find out if it was Ralph's intention, but it made Pelt draw his gun. It wasn't the speed that surprised Calum, he'd expected that, more the overpowering noise as Pelt's Colt exploded. He watched, stunned, made a grab for his own revolver. He saw Ralph clutching his stomach, legs buckling as he staggered backwards, exhausted, looking for an invisible chair to die in.

Pelt fired again, and before Calum had time to action his gun, he felt the hot, dark hammer-punch high on the side of his head.

As Calum collapsed sideways into the side of the bar, the saloon doors crashed apart. Ethan stood in the doorway, both hands steady, cradling a big Remington.

He yelled at Pelt. 'Stop. No more, gunman.'

As the murderous silence descended, Ethan glared. 'If that Colt doesn't hit the floor in three seconds, you'll be taken out with half the back wall.'

It took Pelt no more than a fraction to take on the look in Ethan's eyes. He held out his hand and let the Colt slip from his grasp.

As Ethan moved towards him, Pelt saw the tremor in the nerves of Ethan's face; saw Budge Gourley move to block the swing doors.

'If you see so much as a louse move, kill him, Budge,' Ethan called over his shoulder.

Ethan stepped quickly to his brother's body. He caught the eye of Bella, who was now standing near. 'Get a doctor,' he snapped. 'Take more than five minutes, an' I'll bury you myself.'

With eyes fixed on Calum, Ethan raised himself, and took a few steps backwards. He moved close to Pelt, so close he smelled the gunman's sweet hair-oil. 'I don't know you, but I know what you are. Those two were cattlemen. Not gunfighters.'

Ethan lashed out with his foot, kicking Pelt's Colt across the floor of the saloon. He held out the Remington, turning it in his fingers, pushing the stock deep into Pelt's midriff. 'Take it,' he said. 'Take the gun.'

The men's eyes were locked, as Ethan breathed in real close. 'I'm no gunfighter either, but then again, I'm not a cattleman.'

Ethan backed off a short step. 'That's a single-action .44 Remington. The only way you're gettin' out of dyin' is to shoot me with it. Go ahead.'

Nothing flickered in Pelt's face, and Ethan knew that nothing would. He was acknowledging the mask of a professional gunman.

It was only when the barman's sweaty, trembling hand dropped a glass that a thin smile worked its way across Pelt's lips. Ethan's shoulder moved, but from him there was no thin smile. He remained impassive, waiting for the first curl of Pelt's blood to appear.

When it did, he took back his gun and stepped away. His Bowie knife was thrust low and fatal under Pelt's gun belt.

The gunman showed a run of bloodied teeth as he crumpled to the floor. 'Too close,' he hissed. 'I shoulda known.'

As Ethan went back to Callum, a voice challenged from behind him. Ethan turned to see Chew Heddon. He was in the doorway, standing beside Budge.

'Now, you're on my land, cowboy, an' it's murder, as well as horse-thievin'.' The town's sheriff was aiming a shotgun directly at Ethan.

Ethan swore, turned his attention to Calum. 'I'm tendin' to my brother, Heddon. He's not dyin' because a your stupidity.'

'From where I'm standin, you're in no position to be shoutin' the odds,' the sheriff croaked.

Ethan pulled off his battered Stetson, and rubbed his forehead. 'No, Sheriff. From where *you're* standin', there's a gun ready to shoot your spine away.'

Heddon's jaw dropped. He shuddered as the pressure of Budge's gun bit into the small of his back.

7
Next In Line

Seeing the town's sheriff under close watch from Budge, two of the townspeople got shakily to their feet. 'Ain't these boys, Sheriff,' one of them came out with. 'We saw it all. That's an outa town gunman we never seen afore.'

Budge looked at the faces around him. He nodded at a Big Log cowboy who was sitting with one of the saloon girls. 'You, mister. Get up.'

The cowboy insolently drained his glass, then as Ethan turned to have a look at him, he pushed himself up from the table.

Budge snapped at him. 'Before the night's out, you'll be tellin' Barton Ringwood what happened here. Tell the Sheriff.'

The cowboy nodded in the direction of Pelt's crumpled body. 'I seen him before. Don't rightly recall where. He was on the prod. Plugged Ralph Bones, then he shot Wheat there.' He looked towards Calum.

'Right so far, get on with it,' Budge pressed, impatiently.

'That's when Geronimo comes bustin' in, a whoopin' an' a hollerin'.' The man smirked wryly at Ethan. 'Sweet, it was, Sheriff. Offers the gunman that .44 he's packin', then spikes him with a big huntin' blade.'

The cowboy looked from Ethan to Callum, then back at Heddon. 'Unless you're gonna arrest someone for suicide, Sheriff, you'd best get back to your bottle.'

The Big Log cowboy sat down again, sniggering contemptuously with the saloon's regular customers.

Ethan looked around him, anxious and weary. 'This place ain't fit for a dog,' he muttered and pointed to the street. With her tail between her legs, Elky padded off to sit under the swing doors.

Budge emptied Heddon's shotgun. 'You ain't qualified enough for this,' he said. 'Get back to your hole.'

As Heddon sloped across the darkened street, Ethan stepped up beside him.

He spoke softly. 'The buzzards are still feedin' off someone who tried to bushwhack me, an' lyin' in there's a man who's slung his guns once too often. They were both hired by Ringwood, an' you know it. Me? I'm still kickin'. Don't it make you wonder, Sheriff, whether you're on the right side? The way Ringwood's stackin' things up, you ain't far off bein' next.'

Ethan turned back to the saloon as Bella entered with the town doctor.

Budge moved away, and the doctor kneeled beside Calum. He thumbed the stricken man's eyelids and looked closely at the head wound. 'Cerebral concussion. He'll live. If you can bring him to the surgery, I'll clean and dress that wound. Just get him to rest up for a day or two.'

Budge nodded at Ethan. 'I'll get a wagon. Then we'll take him back to S River.'

Towards the north end of town, several two-storey buildings lay back from the main street. In the deep shadow of one white-painted portico, a shingle hung. It read simply, JUDGE ROWSE MALLARD.

In a downstairs room of the house, Chew Heddon was making his plea. 'I need more backin' for this, Judge. He's shootin' the place up now. I heard him say Wheat was his brother. That means they're brothers.'

Mallard looked closely at Heddon, contemplated the end of his fat cigar. 'I can understand Barton Ringwood's concern about you, Sheriff.'

'This ain't nothin' to do with Mr Ringwood, Judge. One a them Wheats is a horse-thief, an' he's just killed a man in a public buildin'.'

The Judge shook his head. 'One of the advantages of my town and county standing, Sheriff, is that I'm usually kept well-informed. From what I hear, the horse-stealing lacks measure. As for the shooting, well, I'm not issuing an arrest warrant for what I already know to be self-defence on the part of Ethan Wheat.' Heddon was visibly shaken as Mallard continued, 'You seem to have conveniently forgotten that one of Calum Wheat's men was shot dead, Sheriff. Sometimes, it's prudent for the law to merely observe nature's course. Watch the biter get bit.'

Heddon attempted to interrupt, but Mallard held up his plump, smooth hand.

'Sorry Sheriff, but that's the long and the short of it. Furthermore, it's the story you can take out to Barton Ringwood the next time you're summoned. Now if you don't mind, it's getting late.'

As Heddon stepped back into the night, he thought on the warning of Ethan Wheat. There was a jar of pine-top waiting for him back at the jail. But that was looking like the only comfort in Chew Heddon's immediate future.

There were lights, shining thinly from the dust-caked windows of the Boulder Hotel. Heddon stopped, looked up to the fronting boardwalk as he passed. He'd changed his mind about going back to his office and the jail, and he was avoiding the saloon. He rubbed his mouth with the back of his hand, felt the few pennies, low in his pants' pocket. Apart from aimless cowhands, the main street was deserted. He stepped up to the front door of the hotel, hesitated a moment, then entered. A bell pinged over the door, rousing the listless clerk.

The clerk raised his hand. 'Sheriff,' he said. 'I was just comin' over to the jail. Barton Ringwood's upstairs. Says he wants to see you.'

Heddon just stared at the clerk. He had nothing to say. He licked his parched lips, felt the first shiver of the night creep through him.

'Got any mail pockets, there?' he said, thickly.

The clerk shuffled beneath his small reception counter and held out an envelope for the sheriff.

Without a word, Heddon took it and turned his back on the clerk. He removed his metal star of office and pushed it into the fold of thick paper. He handed it back to the clerk and said. 'You make sure Ringwood gets this. He can do with it whatever he wants. I don't give a damn.'

With that, Heddon left the hotel. It was still a few hours away from first light when he arrived at the shambles of his office. He stashed a few belongings and took a handful of papers from his desk drawer. There were two jars of pine-top in the small cell and he rolled them together, cuffing the handles.

He left the lamp burning and went out the rear door of the jail. He walked along the alley behind, until he came to the livery stable. The stable was in pitch darkness and he had to flip a match to see. There was a lamp hanging inside the narrow side door and by its glow he saw his ageing mare.

A bad-tempered grey snorted, and Heddon eyed the loose poles that partially closed its pen. Amongst the strewn hay, there were piles of untreated animal skins and one small wooden crate. It contained what looked like two wolf cubs. Their downy jowls were collapsed to the floor, but their eyes moved from side to side at the alien, terrifying world.

As Heddon backed through the door they raised their heads and looked at him accusingly. 'Tough,' he muttered with some feeling. Then he pushed hard at his horse's shoulder, turning sharply from the crudeness of the building.

Within twenty minutes he'd ridden from the town. There'd be no more kowtowing to Barton Ringwood, and it being the end of the month, Youngsville owed him nothing.

Barton Ringwood stared angrily at Heddon's sullied, five-point star. He'd slept badly as he always did when he was away from Big Log. It was near sun-up and he considered his first cigar of the day, There was a tentative knock at the door of his twin room.

'Stop makin' such a damn row. The door's open, come in,' he rasped.

Wallace Suggs stumped in and cast a sorry look at Ringwood's rich surroundings. 'Mornin' Mr Ringwood,' he mumbled.

Ringwood looked at the small dishevelled man. 'What exactly do you do around this town, Suggs?' he asked with disdain.

'Look after the jail, run sheriff's errands. Sometimes get sworn in as deputy. Help with arrestin', sometimes.'

'Hmmm.' Ringwood turned to look out the window. 'Deputy to Heddon when he's, er . . . indisposed, you mean?'

Suggs shuffled around. 'Happens now and again, Mr Ringwood.'

'How d'ya fancy makin' it hapen full time? You get the badge, an' all Heddon's perks.' Ringwood forced a corrupt grin. 'An' I mean all of 'em, Sheriff Wallace Suggs.'

Suggs looked around the room, unsure of himself. 'Where *is* Chew?'

'He's just resigned. I believe he's heading south to Mexico. The badge is yours if you want it, Suggs. Here, take it with you. We can get you sworn in later in the day.'

Ringwood picked up the badge of office and flicked it casually at the new lawman. 'Go on, try it for size. Get yourself fixed up with a mount while you're about it.'

Suggs caught the badge and rubbed it on the seat of his pants. 'Yes sir, Mr Ringwood. I won't be lettin' you down.'

As Ringwood ushered Suggs from the room, he patted him on the shoulder. 'Remember, Sheriff. You're employed by the town, and I *am* the town.'

As soon as Suggs was gone, Ringwood opened the door to the adjoining room. 'Come in, Rafer. Now we can talk,' he said, urgently.

The man that entered was in the same mould as Mallen Pelt, but twice the size and twice as smart. He remained standing, while Ringwood sat heavily in a chair.

Ringwood pressed the fingertips of both hands together, looked at Rafer Tymes. 'There's not a lot a time, so listen up,' he said. 'There's a fight comin' my way. I thought I was going to avoid it, but things have sort of conspired against me. Your job is to run down S River ranch. That'll be all its stock, the ranch house, and anyone who stands in your way. Crude, but effective. Fast and final. I've got men out at Big Log when you need 'em. I'll pay you a thousand dollars. Half now, half later. You understand?'

'That's a pretty clear picture.' Tymes spoke calmly, chose his words carefully. 'You pay me in *full*, when the job's done. If anything happens to me, you keep your money. If not, you pay me two thousand dollars. Do *you* understand, Mr Ringwood?'

Ringwood gulped, paled a little at Tymes's offer. 'Perhaps you've heard of Mallen Pelt?' he asked.

'I've heard of him, yeah. Our paths have never crossed. I hear he's real good with a gun.'

'*Was*, Rafer, *was*. One of the hazards of your business, I guess. *His* path crossed with someone who was just that bit better,' Ringwood said, cuttingly.

Tymes nodded. 'It's no secret that there's always someone better. It's being aware of who they are, having the edge, that keeps you alive.'

Ringwood's eyes narrowed. 'You won't be needing an edge for the job I want done right now. All you'll need is an eye for a trail and a fast horse.'

8
A Roan Horse

Ten miles south of Youngsville, the range broke gently from the foothills of the Sangre de Christos. After a hunting moon, the first streaks of silver-blue fight cut the giant New Mexican sky.

Since leaving town, Chew Heddon had fretted on his predicament for nearly two hours. Up against Calum Wheat's brother, Ringwood's hired gun hadn't lived long. And if the dead bushwhacker had also been hired by Ringwood, perhaps it was time to choose another side. Choose another side or get the hell away from Santa Rosa.

It was on the still, crystal air that he heard the far-off bark of the dog. Only then did he see the wagon and horses on the horizon. They'd swung east into range-land; he swung west, into foothills, never once looking back.

As the sun started its long climb, Heddon reined in. It was time to water the horse and for himself to tap one of the jars. He dismounted and let the mare sink its nose into the fast, shallow run of the Chama. Uncuffing the pine-top, he raised the jar to his lips, trembled as the raw spirit caught the back of his throat.

There was no pain as the bullet from a big-bore rifle tore into his chest. He never even heard the sharp report that followed, or the echo that crashed away from a distant scrubby bluff.

Heddon's lifeless body arched backwards down into the water. The old mare nickered. It twitched its head at the pungent contents of the shattered jar, shied from the billowing reddish swirl.

Budge Gourley turned sharply to Ethan. 'What the hell was that?'

'Rifle. South, it sounded like. Someone shootin' their breakfast, maybe.'

Ethan was lying in a rumble-wagon. Calum lay next to him, his bandaged head pillowed in a pile of flour sacks. Four horses trailed behind on long reatas.

They were nearing S River, watching thin strands of woodsmoke stretching lazily from the ranch house.

Calum groaned. 'You'll be lookin' after the ranch for a day or two, Ethan. A day in bed should see me all right.' He closed his eyes again.

Budge looked back at Ethan. 'Half an hour, boys. I wonder if Marge can see us?'

Calum managed a thin grin. 'Yeah, she'll be watchin' an' worryin' Budge. More for you than her brothers, I'll bet.'

Ethan gently nudged his brother. 'Quieten up, Cal. Count yourself out for a while. With Budge's help, I'll take care a things.'

'That's what I'm worried about.' Calum opened his eyes again. 'Barton Ringwood'll be spinnin' like a flea on a hot plate. You've already killed two of his men. He'll be sendin' in more.'

Ethan sat more upright, rubbed the small of his back. 'If he dares come to the ranch, we'll fight him from there. But don't fret, nothin's gonna happen for a while. While that thick head of yours is mendin', I'll be takin' a look around the foothills. Got to find me a horse, don't forget. When I get back, the men from Durango'll be here.'

They moved on to the mile of wagon road that led to the main house. Ethan vaulted from the wagon, walked alongside. 'What size is the herd?' he called up to Budge.

'Nearly a hundred in close, some a' the wily old whitefaces. Out at pasture? Maybe a coupla hundred more. Say, three hundred total.'

Ethan thought on. He wasn't a cattleman himself, but he appreciated Budge's association and allegiance. But Ethan knew there was trouble looming. Although in the name of Marge, the ranch was still family. For as long as it took, he'd be needed to carry the fight against Ringwood and Big Log.

With his head-wound causing frequent relapses, Calum couldn't put up much of a fight. For the first twenty-four hours, and with Nate Starling's help, Marge was able to prepare the ranch. They checked on victuals, everything from bullets to beans. If Ringwood planned an assault, then he wouldn't find S River in need.

Ethan was needing a horse; he wasn't well-suited to cow-ponies. He spoke to Budge, and early the following morning packed cheese, meat pies and tinned peaches into a small rig. He took a rope, loose halter and a saddle blanket.

Budge and Nate organized the hands to ride herd. They rode day and night, some to the pasture at the end of the valley, and a few kept watch on the more domesticated, close-grazing whitefaces. It was mostly for reassurance. They believed Ringwood to be reeling from his set-backs, needing time to think out a more successful strategy.

There were hard, stubborn qualities to the land close-bordering the Sangre de Christos. But Budge was right. Thirty miles west of S River ranch, Ethan found a small herd of wild horses. They were drifting to the spills of the Pecos River, where there was summer graze in the brome and rye grass.

It was under the first break of early light and Ethan felt icy rivers of sweat running down his neck and across his shoulders. The silence was overpowering and his heart thumped in fast, aching spasms. He wouldn't move because a blue-roan stallion was suddenly standing off the herd. It trotted stiff-legged to within thirty yards of where Ethan was crouched, arrogant in its ownership and command. It raised its huge, steely coloured head towards him, but Ethan held every nerve tight. It was an instinctive way of hunting and he could remain that way for hours if he had to.

The stallion's eyes were mean with challenge and the inside of its flaring nostrils were swollen-red and gleaming. It curled its lips against huge, yellow molars to let out one screaming whinny and Ethan withered. He'd never felt such emotion from a physical presence and against all reason he rose to face the wildness.

The stallion broke and whirled towards his small band of mares. They fled before him, running wildly in swerving files through the grass and low scrub.

After a full mile, and with the mares in continuing flight, the stallion muscled himself into a dramatic, dust-raising halt. He faced back towards Ethan, stamping his forelegs and branding the hard ground with his fearful hooves.

Ethan kneeled and laid the palm of one hand against the soil. He ran a sensitive finger around the rim of a hoof-print, looked hard at the blanket of dust coiling low in the distance. He'd found his horse, and in two or three days he would be back at S River.

Rafer Tymes was a man who liked to move fast. He'd make his $2,000 in a few days, rather than string it out.

Concealed by high scrub he sat his big horse, looking thoughtfully across the S River longhorns. He chewed his lip, as one of the Big Log riders reined in alongside him.

'Five *vaqueros, señor.*' Gila said. 'They carry many guns. Look like they expectin' trouble.'

'Yeah, I've noticed,' Tymes replied. 'And it's not by chance. Five against three's the odds you can die by.'

It was a few moments before Gila spoke. 'Then we ride west. There's a small herd a whiteface an' some pretty Poll Durhams. Close to ranch house, but not much guard left; they mostly here. What you think?'

'You could be right. We'll take a look.' Tymes swung his horse, waving to Gila's partner. 'It's nearly five, getting late. At least them S River boys won't choke on breakfast beans.'

9
Attack on S River

Close to the ranch house in the sheltered river bend, Budge and Nate Starling were hidden in the willow-stands. They stood opposite each other playing rumblypeg; flinging clasp knives into the ridged bark between their legs.

'You're the only one I'd trust this with, Nate,' Budge said, grinning. 'You've a good eye. Years ago me an' Ethan used to play it. That's before we realized the potential of a miss.'

The men laughed easily, then Nate squinted over Budge's shoulder. 'I think we should just slide down, slow and easy.'

Budge's eyes narrowed straight at Nate. 'What's up? What you seen?'

'Three riders. They're a ways off yet, but headin' this way. Let's reckon it's Big Log.'

Budge rolled into the shallow muddied scrape that

53

edged the river bend. He turned his head toward Nate. 'I'll cover the herd from downstream, you take the upper bend, Nate. We'll have 'em in a crossfire. What do you think?'

'Yeah, good. You got plenty of ammunition?'

'Enough.'

Nate nodded. 'If they come in file, take the first one, Budge. If not, take the one nearest you. I'll hold up until you fire. Take care.'

Levering shells into chambers, both men crawled to their positions. Earlier in the day they'd slapped their horses back to the ranch yard. If there'd been no trouble, Marge would have led them back at sundown.

For many minutes the silence was broken only by the murmur of water and the thump of their hearts. From nearly a mile away they watched. The mounted figures of Rafer Tymes and his men rose and fell as they rode through the undulating gullies.

Gila's eyes quartered the land ahead. He noted the willow stands, waiting for any sudden bird flight; but they were long gone. He rode cautiously ahead of Tymes and Peachy Pump, the other Big Log rider. He held up a hand and Tymes drew in close.

'If they are there, they'll be near willow,' the Mexican said, looking for the slightest movement.

Tymes clasped tight-gloved hands to the horn of his saddle. 'Maybe. Can't see any horses,'

Gila looked uncertain. 'But horses don't carry guns, *señor*. Something tell me to ride on.'

Tymes caught the sense of foreboding. 'We'll ride *in*,

fast. Turn from the willows, push the beeves out ahead of us. If we move fast enough, we'll outrun anyone on foot.'

'It's outrunnin' a big bullet that worries me,' Pump said, nudging his horse alongside Gila. 'If there's anyone at the ranch they'll hear the gunfire.'

'Can't be much more'n the girl out there, an' Ringwood says to leave her well alone.' Tymes looked at Gila inquisitively.

Gila shrugged. 'I think perhaps the boy, Festus.'

Tymes gripped his reins. 'Let's see if there's any guns in them willows.'

Budge sighted the riders, nestled his elbows in the bankside crust. Passing his old .44 Henry from left to right, back to left, he was breathing relaxed and shallow.

Nate clenched his teeth, rubbed at his eyes. Across the bend in the course of the river he could see where Budge would be lying, see where the tip of his rifle would be. He focused again on the lead rider as the horsemen came towards them. He hoped Budge wouldn't leave it that late before firing. He didn't want four men shooting over his head.

At 300 yards, Gila spurred his mount into a full gallop. Tymes and Pump spread either side.

When the men were close to 200 yards, the first of the Poll Durhams raised its shaggy head. Its bellow was immediately picked up and the herd began its nervous movement.

Nate's eyes flicked from his rifle sights to the herd,

then to Budge's position. It was becoming obvious; the approaching horsemen were going to grip the small herd of frightened animals in the river bend. There was no way out; they'd panic and mill, then they'd be run out, fast.

Nate realized that that was when Budge would open fire, before the riders ran the herd into the range, With a bit of luck the herd would remain contained and, in the crossfire, Nate and Budge would take out the rustlers.

Budge recognized Pump and Gila, the top hands at Big Log, but he'd never seen the big man before, the one taking middle position.

As all three riders rode into the open end of the natural enclosure, Budge fired. The single shot cracked across the open ground and Peachy Pump jerked from his saddle.

Gila instinctively fell forward away from the gunshot, his legs and one arm groping at his horse's belly and saddle rig. Nate squeezed the trigger, watched as his bullet took the Mexican in the back of his neck.

Rafer Tymes swore, then calmly swung his big horse. He rode straight for the herd, seeking cover in the wild seething brown mass.

Pump was on all fours. He was staring down, watching, as the ground between his outstretched fingers swam in and out of focus. The pain of the bullet lodged deep in his side brought short convulsive breaths, then dark insensibility as his arms collapsed. His last sensation was the warm fouled dirt as it pressed into the gape of his mouth.

For a few seconds the fear of dying kept Gila clutched to his saddle, the side of his horse. Then his hands and legs gave way. His body trailed, one foot twisted hopelessly in the stirrup. The pulse of blood from his shattered neck marked the pummelled ground as his horse tore fearfully away.

Budge and Nate turned their guns on Tymes as he pulled at his horse. The resolute gunman was looking for them, his one free hand seeking a target for his rifle.

The S River men held their fire. The Poll Durhams were bellowing, some rearing, thrashing the thick air with their hooves. Tymes was lost in the cloud, but he was forcing his way to the back of the graze, to where the river took its boundary curve.

Budge had one fleeting glance at the moving gunman and managed a shot, close above the lashing horns of the cattle. It caught Tymes, but took no more than a chew of flesh from his upper arm.

Tymes kicked into the fast-running water. The blood ran into the clutch of his hand, and as his fingers lost control he dropped his rifle. His horse slashed its forelegs at the current, squealed as Tymes urged it forward on to the bank, then the open range.

As Tymes spurred the horse south, he heard rapid fire from the willow-stands now behind him. He clenched his teeth against the pulsating pain in his shoulder, but he never felt the expected punch in the middle of his back.

Nate stepped into the neck of the graze. The cattle were moving nearer, sensing the escape route. He fired low above their bobbing heads, then Budge came running. Together they pumped bullets into the air and into the ground to head off the herd.

They walked forward, slowly packing the herd into a crushed but contained bunch. Sharing the same thought, the two men stopped, looked repelled at each other. There wasn't much left of Gila and Peachy Pump, just razed bundles, mangled and bloodless. The dead men's horses had crossed the river, fleeing west, back in the direction of Big Log Ranch.

Rafer Tymes made it to the safety of the foothills; half-way between the S River and Big Log ranches. He cleaned his ripped shoulder, stuffed the lacerated flesh with damp moss and willow-herb. He rested up, thinking over the ambush from which he'd narrowly escaped. Barton Ringwood had promised more men if he needed them. Well, he did now. Taking on S River was more than a neighbourly quarrel and the bodies were mounting.

The gunman winced, closed his eyes. On Ringwood's account, he'd rest up a bit in Youngsville. From now on, he could be working real hard for his money.

10

The Men from Durango

In the days that followed, a nervous calm shadowed S River.

Calum was stirring, making frustrated noises, but any exertion hit his head like a hammer. Likewise in the Big Log camp, the ramrod, Moss, was still feeling the same way.

Although instigated by Barton Ringwood, both sides were reeling from the fighting. The way things were shaping up, the next step would be close to an all-out range war.

The Big Log outfit had the men already. They just needed to cast the final play. But it was clear at S River, that *they'd* need Ethan and his men from Durango.

Nate Starling had quickly moved the cattle in from the far pasture, and four hands had stayed on to watch over the herd.

Each day Elky would sit for hours pining by the willows, eyes locked on the eastern horizon. Then as dusk fell she'd return to the house, ever hopeful for Ethan's return.

Since the fight with Rafer Tymes, Budge and Marge had drawn close. They'd both felt the need for someone to share their anxiety. They'd known each other for many years, but it was only now that mutual feeling became obvious.

'Do you know what we're supposed to do now, Marge?'

'I know what's going to happen. Is that what you're thinking about?'

'Maybe, yeah. Only there's never been much beyond the *happenin'* before, for me to think about.'

Marge looked suitably wounded. 'Oh, there has been a *before* then?'

Budge felt the colour rising from his feet. 'Well, yes, ma'am. You don't spend time out here, without. . . .'

'I think *without*'s as far as you need to go, Budge.' With a finger against his lips, Marge stopped him from any further talking.

When darkness descended across S River, the couple were sitting on the stoop of the house. They had their arms around each other, but drew fragile comfort from their established affection. They listened to the whirr of nightjars around the willows, watched the moon shining on the snowy tips of the distant mountains.

'Do you think Ethan *will* be back soon?' Marge asked.

'Soon,' Budge said. 'Maybe tomorrow; and Cal will be

up and about within a day or two.'

'I'm scared Budge. Scared for when Ethan finds out what's happened here. There's how many men dead already? There's no law. We can't stand up to Ringwood and his men on our own. He'll send more now.'

Budge thought about it. 'Well, at least something good's come out of it, Marge.' He squeezed her hand and laughed. We'll just have to make sure we stay alive.'

He looked into her face. 'Come on, think of the silver lining. There's four of the hands remaining. Ethans coming with his men from Durango. Calum's getting better, and there's *me*, don't forget. We're big enough to take on Barton Ringwood. If not, then we'll surrender, ride off into the sunset.'

Marge pulled a wry face. 'Why can't we send someone to Carlsbad, even Las Cruces? They've got county sheriff's offices. Surely they're beyond the corruption of Ringwood?'

'I wonder if *anyone* south of the llano's beyond that, Marge.'

Budge got up and stood facing the Sangre de Christos. 'When all this is over Marge, and it will be, do you think we could. . . ?'

Marge moved to stand beside him. 'Yes, Budge, I *do* think we could. I think there's a very *good* chance.'

The Tahl-Tan bear-dog leapt for the door of the ranch house. She sprang up, pawing frantically at the big wooden crossbar. Her barking got Calum from his bed, but Marge was already there, peering through the window-shutters.

'What's going on, Marge?' he shouted, wincing from the dull ache across his temples.

'There's a group of riders. I don't recognize them. Are they Big Log or Ethan's men?' Marge turned to see Callum awkwardly ramming cartridges into a shotgun.

'Only one way to find out, Sis. If they're Ethan's men they'll just sit. If not, they'll be expectin' this.'

With one hand, Calum slid the crossbar from its racks. He unlocked the door and lifted the big latch. He thought for a second, then handed Marge the shotgun. 'We can't afford trouble just yet. I'd better find out who they are, what they want. If anything happens, remember I'm the good guy.' Calum took a deep breath and opened the door.

Calum was faced by five men. They sat their horses, trail-weary and ragged, but in control.

He looked at each of the five inscrutable faces, spoke to no one in particular. 'I'm Calum Wheat, and this is S River. I take it you ain't lost. What's your business?'

One of the horsemen lifted his hat and puffed his cheeks. 'We followed the river. Got a bit confused out there by the patch of willow. If we'd followed them bends, as Ethan said, we'd a turned tail back to Arizona.'

A slow relieved smile, broke across Calum's face. 'I ain't normally given to piety, mister, but thank God you've arrived.'

Calm, but tired in the saddle, the man responded.

'My name's Judd Finch,' he said. He looked to the left of Calum's shoulder. 'That'll be your an' Ethan's sister Marge, aiming the shotgun at me?'

Calum nodded. 'Yeah. Ethan ain't here though. He's off catchin' himself a horse.'

Finch's men looked at each other and grinned. Then they backed their horses a pace or two, touched their guns.

Hurrying across the yard, Budge and Nate Starling were buckling on their gunbelts. The other hands stood back. They were crowded in the bunkhouse doorway, nervously tugging at their long johns, hats and boots.

Calum held up his hand. 'It's Ethan's men, Budge. This is Judd Finch. Take 'em to the bunkhouse. Nate, will you get their horses tended? Big food all round. Wait there a second,' he added.

Calum went back into the house and returned a few moments later, tossed a bottle of McCoys to Finch. 'Lay the dust, Judd. Then we'll talk of fly-swattin'.'

Barton Ringwood returned from Youngsville to find his son lolling in a rawhide hammock. It was approaching midday, and Festus appeared to be half asleep in the shade of the veranda. He looked up when his father walked up the steps, groaned and rolled unsteadily to his feet.

'Hey, ol' goat, where ya been? Only one thing'll keep a man that long in Pokesville.'

Ringwood eyed the young man, who'd obviously been drinking. Festus's face was flushed and damp, his hair sweated thickly to his head.

'Get yourself sobered up, then you can talk if you've anything to say,' Ringwood said, sadly.

'I'm as sober as I need be.' Festus glared at his father. 'Not that you'd notice, but I ain't a kid any more.'

Ringwood nodded. 'Yeah, that's the cryin' shame of it, Festus. Tell it to the bottle you've been suckin' on.'

Lurching, Festus followed his father into the ranch house. 'I've got summat to say to you all right. Summat real interestin' 'bout that Ethan Wheat. The one's been givin' you all the trouble.'

Ringwood pulled off his Stetson, yawned and sat heavily in his big fireplace chair. He stretched his legs and stared challengingly at Festus. 'You got something to tell me about him, you tell it now, while you're still on your feet.'

Festus leered. 'I'm the one that's standin' Daddy. Before you drop off, listen to this.'

Ringwood watched as Festus licked his lips in anticipation of his story.

'I took a ride out to the S River line-shack, the one up near where the Chama joins the Pecos. Added a little something to the water. Should sweeten things up, when it washes down to the pools.'

'I know you been doin' that, Festus. But they ain't gonna be runnin' cattle up there, you young fool. It's south to El Paso they'll be goin', if they're goin' anywhere. Anyway, what of it?' Ringwood asked.

'I saw Wheat. He was in a rig, coming back from the timberline.'

Ringwood raised his chin, waited for Festus to continue.

'He had a horse, a big roan stallion running along behind. Reckon he'd been on a chase.'

'That's interestin' son, but don't add up to a lot. So he's got himself a new mount?'

Festus's eyes widened. 'Yeah, but that's not all though. I saw riders comin' through the valley. They were followid the river, east. It goes right the way to River S, an' they weren't no punchers. By the look of 'em they'd rode a long way. I reckon them Wheats are organizin' some reinforcements, Big Daddy.'

Ringwood rubbed his temples with his fingertips. 'They weren't together then, Wheat and those riders?'

'No. Wheat would have been half a day behind 'em. What do you make a that?'

'Don't rightly know what to make of it. But you could be right Festus. It'd be what I'd do in the circumstances.'

Festus laughed. 'I thought you *had* done it. An' already lost most of 'em to Wheat's guns.'

Then his expression suddenly changed. He looked keenly at his father. 'There was somethin' about those men.'

'Whaddya mean?' Ringwood grunted.

'The way they rode . . . tight . . . determined . . . quiet like. If they are musterin' at S River, you're gettin' up to your snout in trouble.'

Ringwood closed his eyes. 'If they're squarin' up for a fight, we'll give 'em one, Festus. There'll be no need for you to put yourself in danger, if that's what's worryin' you.'

The rancher was tired. His head throbbed with

tiredness and the oppressive heat. He'd rode in from Youngsville, totting up the Big Log deaths. First, Charlie Lemon, then Mallen Pelt. Chew Heddon had resigned his office, nearly made it to the timberline. Now his top hand, Gila, and a wrangler were shot down at S River. Rafer Tymes had narrowly escaped, but he'd come close to meeting his maker.

He sensed a closeness and opened his eyes to find Festus leaning over him.

The boy whispered threateningly. 'If this affair ain't sorted out soon, Big Daddy, *I'll* arrange things. The only one left to tell about it will be the little Wheat filly.'

With that, Festus stomped out of the ranch house. Ringwood was shaken, and he dragged himself out of his chair. He stood in the dorway and shouted for Albert Cheeseman, the old make-good man.

Within moments Cheeseman appeared. He was overalled, holding a pitchfork splattered with livery manure.

Ringwood stood with hands on hips. 'Tell Moss to get back on his feet. Turn him out of his sack if you have to. Get him here, right now.'

Cheeseman piked the ground with his fork and stomped to the bunkhouse.

Ringwood glared uneasily around the yard of the ranch. When Moss appeared, he waved him forward, impatiently.

'How many days you need to mend, Moss? Don't answer. Send out a rider or do it yourself, I don't care how. But get Dutch Joe here. I also want Doughy

Seaton, Minch Eaves and Little Copper.'

Moss looked suddenly interested. 'Somethin' happenin', Mr Ringwood?'

'Yeah, sounds like plenty. You ride into town, pick up Rafer Tymes. He'll be in my rooms at the hotel. The men can leave their old crowbaits behind. Get 'em to pick good fresh mounts from the corral. I'll supply all the food an' ammunition you're likely to need.'

'Likely to need?' Moss repeated, questioningly.

'That's right, Moss. Ethan Wheat made a mistake in givin' you that ugly mug. Only you ain't gonna make the same mistake. I've got two hundred dollars says there's soon gonna be an S River drive to El Paso. You get my meanin'?'

Moss put a hand to the stained bandage that ran across his face. 'Yes, Mr Ringwood. From now on, none a them Wheats or their kind are gonna walk away. I'll get the boys in. We should make town by dusk.'

Ringwood went back into the ranch house. He entered his den and walked over to a bookcase. He ran the back of his hand along a row of leather-bound books, pulled out a folded, illustrated print and flattened it across his desk. It was a map of New Mexico and Texas. With his finger, he traced a line from San Antonio and Del Rio. East of El Paso, he paused at the Santa Rosa range-lands. The rancher grinned, private and covetous. There was a small crude pictograph of a railway platform and its nameboard. It said simply, RINGWOOD.

At S River, raked against his bolster, Calum Wheat was

studying the same quarter of a similar map. His head-wound had repaired well, but he was still irritable from being laid up, not yet saddle-ready.

Late the previous evening, Ethan had returned to much hullabaloo from Elky, and to the relief and pleasure of his brother and sister. He'd spent an hour, jawing and ribbing with his friends from Durango.

The roan was much admired. Nate Starling thought it must be one of the finest stallions south of Montana.

Now it was early the morning after, and Judd Finch and his men were getting familiar with the ranch layout.

Calum was making a show of being on the mend, but he was crabby, straining to get to grips with Ringwood's forceful oppression. His dulled eyes showed the pain he was occasionally suffering, as with Ethan, he speculated on Ringwood's next move.

'He knows the herd's all we got. We lose that, an' there's nothin'. We won't be able to hold on to the ranch. Him an' Gill Morrow will see to that. You've got to get the cattle away. Drive 'em to El Paso, and quick, before they hit us again.'

'How do I get 'em there without the whole valley knowing?'

'I've been thinkin' of that. Look, I'll show you.'

Calum moved a finger across the map. 'The way I've planned it, and if you avoid the trail, it's no more than a hundred miles from here to the railhead. You've got to run 'em east, across the top of the valley. After ten miles turn south, hug the foothills. That'll be a tough stretch. Real scrub, thirty, maybe forty miles of it.'

Calum peered more closely at the map. 'There's a pass at Hueco. It'll be narrow and stony, but at this time a year you should be able to get through. That's when the picnic ends though. Accordin' to this, there's no shorter way. You'll have to cross Blanca Flats.'

Ethan looked concerned. 'How far?'

'About twenty miles. There'll be water-holes; take Elky to look for 'em. It looks like none runnin' fresh till you reach the Rio Grande. Then you can swim 'em across, somewhere between Berino and La Union. From there on it's twenty miles a grass to El Paso. Try an' put back some a the lard.'

Ethan looked doubtful. 'Do you know anyone that's ever gone that way?'

'No. I've heard tell of part of it, but that's what maps are for, Ethan. We've never wandered off the main trail before.'

Ethan nodded at the map, grinned feebly. 'That's because there's Apache east of Blanca Flats, Cal.'

'The only Indians left there are the ones too old or sick for the government to bother about relocating. They don't give trouble any more. Not as much as Ringwood's men will if they catch your wind.'

'No alternative then?'

The nerves in Calum's jaw twitched. ' 'Course there's an alternative Ethan. It's up to you. You don't have to make the drive. You can stay here or ride off,' he said testily.

'Sorry Cal. It's just that cow-pokin's not what I'm best at.'

'It's your gun that's needed, brother. Leave the herd

to Budge or Judd Finch.'

Marge, who was standing in the doorway, listening, took a step forward. 'You're sending Budge Gourley on that drive?'

Calum shot a quick, circumspect glance at Ethan before answering his sister. 'He's the only 'Budge' around these parts, Marge. Why?'

Without replying, Marge, turned and disappeared somewhere back into the house.

Ethan raised his eyebrows. 'Did you know?'

Calum smiled. 'Not for sure. I thought she was keeping herself for young Festus Ringwood.'

The brothers chortled good humouredly, then Ethan shook his head.

'That'll be Budge *and* the herd I've got to look after. Think I will need the dog.' He got up and stood looking out the window. 'What do I do when I get to the rail-head?'

'Go to the Cattlemen's Association. Ask for Sam Barston. He's reputable and fair. But don't let on you're desperate. We are, but don't let him know that. Just get the best price you can, Ethan.'

Out near the corral, Ethan saw Elky watching the roan. It was an inquisitive, first daylight encounter. The dog had her belly and tail flat on the ground, ears forward. It was a good sign.

Ethan turned back to Calum. 'You're only desperate when you don't understand; and I think I'm beginning to. I guess you want me to make a cash deal?'

'Yeah. It's the only way. If I present Gil Morrow with anything less than cash, he'll stall. Him an' Ringwood have both got their snouts in the trough. He'll find the slightest excuse to hold things up. Besides, I want to see his face when we pay the mortgage.'

'We won't take less than seven days, Cal. It'll be quicker comin' home, but with that money we'll still have to avoid the cattle trail. Maybe we'll loop east round the salt lakes. Looks like a route on that map a yours.'

Calum's eyes roved across the geographical features. 'It's a prospector's chart for the Sacramentos. It ain't meant to cover the border in close detail. As long as you remember it's due south gettin' there, and due north gettin' back, you won't get lost.'

Ethan seemed satisfied. 'An' I won't be hesitatin' neither. That's why we'll be movin' out at first light tomorrow.'

11

The Trail to Water

Early evening at the back of the Prairie Dust saloon, Festus Ringwood was sipping whiskey. He was in a poker game with Moss, his father's ramrod, a cashiered Texas Ranger named Coney Rimmer and an intrepid street urchin.

The urchin had a bottle of beer in front of him, and a thumb-sized cork in a corner of his mouth. Despite its name, kids didn't grow up in towns like Youngsville, there was never a chance. They hauled their way up to the first set of double figures, then leapt headlong into whatever remained.

Festus was talking to Moss, careless and unguarded. 'How do you know them S River cowboys have rode to El Paso?'

'Your pa had the ranch watched. Saw 'em move out. We meet 'em on the range. Your pa's orders, an' I'm takin' guns.' Moss touched the ridge of gnarled flesh that cut the front of his face. 'I've a score to settle with Wheat.'

Festus looked around the saloon, back to the table. He was unhappy, searching through his fist of cards. Rimmer had been taking money from them for over an hour. 'Who's goin'?' he wanted to know.

Moss touched a card for each name. 'Eaves, Dutch Joe, Doughy an' Little Copper. Rafer Tymes'll join us on the trail.'

'An' I'll join you down there. I wanna see it get done proper this time,' Festus snapped.

Festus knew Rimmer had been cheating. He recognized the sort who thought it their right. He made an almost imperceptible nod at Moss, and moved noiselessly from the table. He stayed away long enough to relieve himself in the adjoining alley.

Impatiently, Rimmer slammed his 'trick' face down on to the table. The drinking-glasses rattled, and he grasped the bottle of sour whiskey. He glanced rudely at Moss.

'Is that pushy kid comin' back? He musta' seen my nines.' He wiped his mouth and nose simultaneously across the sleeve of his ragged coat, adding to the sludge that already crusted his forearm.

Headstrong, Festus came back to the table. He glanced at Moss, then turned on Rimmer. He was pushing for the confrontation, and he nodded provocatively at the clutch of the man's hand. 'One of those cards came from your sleeve, not the pack.'

The Ranger hesitated for a moment, then leaned

forward, ran his fingers around the inside of his boot. He straightened his back, lifted his arm quickly, but Festus was ready and eager, had the advantage. He drove his fingers in hard against the man's neck, watching the face as it twisted down into the card table. There was a clatter on the floor, and Festus bent down and picked up a thin-bladed knife. He flicked it on the table, and pulled the Ranger round on to his front. The man's big front teeth had split his lip, and from his open mouth, blood welled across his yellowing teeth.

Festus could see by the look on Moss's face there was something wrong, and he turned to see two more Rangers advancing towards him. One of them held out a broken sabre, its snapped point waving at his chest. The man shook his head and turned to his colleague.

'We got us a dude, if I ain't mistaken. A dude that's done summat real bad, an' a skinnin' offence if ever I seen one. We could make a saddle blanket from his hide.'

Festus was aware of his standing in Youngsville, and his father's warning about incitement and potential trouble. He swept the glasses, cards, and whiskey bottle from the table. In the instant the Rangers ducked and swung away, he was off. He sprang across a table near the door, and flung himself into the street. Within minutes, he'd disappeared into the shanties and flop-tents at the southern end of town. Even the hard-bitten were reluctant to follow into that den of pollution and depravity.

The Rangers took a long, hard look at Rimmer, then

grabbed at his arms. By the way they dragged him across the floor, Moss was certain that Festus had hit him with a fatal blow. He snarled at them as they pulled the body through the door.

'He had a knife in his boot, and a card up his sleeve.'

Moss tolerated Festus solely because he was the boss's son, could also be tapped for a drink or a small loan until pay-day. Some other time, some other place, Moss would have avoided the wanton youngster. Nevertheless, siding with Festus at the moment could bring a bonus. For Moss, a better deal than incurring a dangerous and temperamental enemy.

The Big Log ramrod didn't take long to find Festus; he'd legged it to the corrals. Disreputable pens, where stolen stock were kept until sharp buyers could be found. In the fast-failing light he was eyeing two unbroken mustangs, one of them a fine chestnut.

As Moss approached, Festus looked up. 'They say chestnuts'll die before tirin',' he said, slow and thoughtful.

Moss could see Festus had something in mind, but let it go. 'What *is* your interest in S River?' he asked.

Festus kept his eyes on the chestnut. 'There's a couple a things I want. They're both being held at the Wheat ranch house.'

Moss leaned against a corral post. 'Let me guess. They'll both be for ridin', and there's six legs between 'em. How'm I doin', Festus?'

Festus turned, quickly. 'I'll pay you a hundred dollars an' you'll need two more men. There's time yet.

You'll be able to catch up with Tymes and the herd well before they reach the railhead.'

'An' when we've delivered, done your dirty work, you'll be meetin' us down in El Paso, will you?' Moss asked doubtfully.

'It's the job at S River I'm payin' for, Moss. Keep that meat lump of a face outa anything else. It's easy enough. One a the Wheats is still laid up. You an' the boys can take care of any that stay back.'

'It's payment I had in mind, Festus. Not what you're wrappin' your legs round. Horses or otherwise.'

Festus pulled out a roll of notes, and peeled them off, one by one. 'There you are, a hundred dollars. It's up to you how you spread it. Just get the job done.'

'You'll be ridin' with us?' Moss asked.

'Yeah, I will. Get your men and move fast. I don't want to be here when those Rangers from the saloon sort out another knife routine.'

As the two men walked, cautious and alert to the far end of the town, Moss was still worried. 'You reckon those new men they've got at S River will all be goin' on the drive?'

'Yeah, that's what they were hired for.'

'How about the law, Festus? Which side we facin'?'

Festus grinned. 'The law gets paid to face the other way. No one's gonna get hurt, but if it don't work out, we can hightail it; ride straight south.' He pulled at a small, flat bottle of whiskey. 'Stop worryin', Moss. This one you can't lose.'

It was a few hours earlier the same day, but ten miles

east of the S River spread.

Ethan Wheat had jigged his roan in close to Budge Gourley. They'd pushed the cattle through the first leg of the drive to El Paso.

'We'll be turnin' south in the mornin', Budge. How about makin' camp? We're away from the main trail, an' there's good beddin' ground.'

'Yeah, let's give 'em another hour. Get in closer to the foothills.'

Ethan nodded in agreement. 'Our first and last camp with much comfort. From first light tomorrow, it'll get tougher. I'm gonna take a ride. See you in a couple of hours.'

For the next hour, Ethan rode ahead. He wanted to catch sight of the land that lay ahead. He knew they'd have to push south, through thirty, forty miles of rugged scrubland. The going would be hard-line, and the herd would quickly lose fat.

The sun had dipped low in the west, but the open range still held the day's warmth. Larks were dropping back to the grassland, behind the slow-moving cattle. The next day, there'd be nothing much but chicken and jack rabbit. But any meaty critter would be safe from the S River cook-pot. In the hot, still air, the pungent smell of the herd would carry for five miles; the shot from a gun, maybe twenty. That was far enough to be picked up by any Big Log riders taking the main trail.

Ethan looked hard at the land. His dog, Elky, lay intelligent and alert, close in to the feet of the roan.

'You're here to find water.' Ethan looked down at the Tahl-Tan. 'Enjoy the view. This time tomorrow when we hit that lot, you'll be earnin' your keep.'

Ethan moved the eager stallion from a walk into a full, unrestrained gallop. There was no exertion or reaching for speed, it was simply notching up, enjoying the moving and exhilaration of its power. Ethan felt the huge muscles pulsing under him; the few miles back to camp easing away under the flying hooves. Looping from left to right, Elky raced beside them, the occasional yip and swerve tracing her excitement and freedom.

Judd Finch's men rode night herd. In the early morning they were relieved by Finch himself, and three S River cowboys.

Ethan didn't take a turn, but on the other hand, he didn't sleep either; there was too much on his mind. He lifted his Stetson from the front of his face.

'Hey, Budge. You awake?'

'Yep,' came the muffled reply. 'I'm lyin' here a-thinkin', watchin' the stars.'

'How much water we carryin'? Ethan asked.

'A canteen each, water-bags, an' two barrels on the wagon. Why?'

'Oh, just wondered. What's that up there, east a bit, three stars in a line?'

'Orion, the Hunter. That's his belt. The other two are his dogs, I think.'

'Hmmm,' Ethan responded, then laughed, quietly. Then there was silence.

The ground-chill clawed at them as they swallowed their eggs, beans and hot biscuits. They ate standing, stamping the ground to get lazy blood moving.

They'd moved the herd south. They were twenty miles – a long day's drive into the barren, scrub; halfway to the pass at Hueco.

There'd been no water. The few holes and sinks were dried out or polluted; thick, muddy-cracked and pocked by the feet of lone hunters.

As usual, Ethan rode ahead. Every now and again Elky would return to join the roan in a slurp from the crown of Ethan's hat. Ethan had already calculated that between the riders, they could, if pushed, dole out a mouthful of water to every head of the herd. Not much, but maybe enough to keep them moving.

It was already approaching noon, and the sun powered down. There was no shade as Ethan faced the shimmering horizon. He'd edged closer to the timberline hoping for a low stream-run, but it appeared a futile detour.

Elky was far ahead when she sniffed the water. But it was another stagnant pool lying at the base of a shaled depression and she was raving with thirst. She plunged her nose to lap at the diseased water, then drank with the recklessness and desperation of finding.

As Ethan approached, the dog's neck muscles were already losing control. He watched helpless as her head lowered. He leaped from his horse, ran, stumbled forward to the edge of the mire as her legs began to buckle.

Elky shivered, swayed gently against his legs. She howled once, then collapsed across his boots. Ethan kneeled to scratch the tight matted hair above her dark muzzle, make soothing noises as he watched her stomach heave with the bilious soup.

The heat was so intense, the pool was still thickening. The overpowering stench of rotting algae was liquefying the roof of Ethan's mouth. He shouted, waved the roan away, then stared dully into Elky's eyes. He pressed his chafed hands into the short warm hair, gently kneeding the collapsed sinews of his Tahl-Tan bear-dog.

He tried to focus, but the shimmering ribbons of heat wound with salt water and filled his eyes. His body convulsed and a tormenting choke clawed its way from deep and concealed within him. He curved to the ground, mercifully crushing life from the suffering of his dog.

When the roan snuffled in again, Ethan grabbed the bridle, pulled his face away from the ground. He dragged thin, rasping spasms from lungs that were hot and charred with dust. The year before he'd lit out for Arizona, Elky had been a birthday present from his father. She was one of six whelps out of a blood-line that hunted bear and beaver high in the Sangre de Christos.

Ethan had nothing to bury or even shroud the dog with. He thought about taking her back to camp; then accepted the shackle of life and death deep in the wasteland. For Elky, maybe only a disguise for her next hunting trip.

On his ride back, Ethan felt the grip of retribution tighten. No one family had the right to crush another.

He'd already considered turning back the herd, but the Wheat family needed the cash from the sale. They'd have to push on, water the cattle from their own barrelled supply, wet 300 tongues with a once-off lifesaver.

The resolve of a final confrontation grew. If he wanted to, Barton Ringwood could set up his own God's Acre in El Paso or back at S River. The way Ethan felt, the difference didn't amount to a hill of beans.

12
Night Steal

In the willow-stands edging the tight curve of water around S River, a man stood holding four horses and three sets of steel spurs. Ahead, in the deep blackness of night, Festus Ringwood, Moss and Minch Eaves stealthily approached the silent ranch house. They avoided the bunkhouse, but at three in the morning, they didn't expect much in the way of watchful activity from any stay-back cowboys.

Eaves led them across the strap of timbered bridge at the rear of the big yard. He faltered at the whirr of a night jar and then again at the creak of willow. There was one guard slumped half-asleep, his gunbelt coiled around the toes of his boots. The man snorted as Eaves advanced, choked as big fingers clamped around his throat. He was already sightless as he twisted into the water below. It would be two or three miles before his body sprawled into the shingle crossing at Ragland.

The three men listened to the hee-haw of a mule, the

answering whinny of a mare in the distance, then made their way slowly along the side of the house. Festus twitched, puffed out his cheeks and brushed his hand across his face. He'd become jumpy, and time was passing. The dark sky was already streaked with the thinnest slivers of first light.

Festus led them to a window that was an inch or so off the sill, but a blind was pulled. Grinding his teeth, he eased up the window with his thumbs, drew the blind to one side. Thin, random light flicked from the rims of crocks and pans and Festus guessed it was the kitchen.

The three men climbed into the house, silently padded their way into the deeper gloom. They slid their hands tentatively along the inner walls, listening for the slightest sound of movement.

With Festus leading, they inched forward. There was a small chair beside the door of one of the rooms, and Festus nudged it with his knee. He stopped, alert for any response, but nothing happened. He touched a shawl or blanket across the back of the chair, and took a gamble.

Using firm but gentle pressure he turned the handle, easing the door slowly inward. Once into the room the light increased slightly, and from the warm, sweet fragrance Festus knew they'd found Marge's bedroom.

Festus knew he'd have to be sure and act fast to prevent an uncontrollable ruckus in the house. He moved further into the room, allowing Eaves and Moss to follow.

In almost total silence the men were spreading themselves for the grab, when a button on Festus's coat slipped into the beaded string of Marge's Apache charm bag. Ethan's present was looped around a foot-post of her bed.

As the string snapped, Marge's small collection of childhood snuggies splattered across the floor. In the taut, choked silence it was enough to raise the dead.

Marge yelled, automatically threw out her arm towards the bedside oil lamp. The glass shattered, its broken shards flying into the far corner of the room.

Festus swore and made a grab for his gun. Eaves and Moss backed off, trying to find the standpoint of a wall.

Marge started yelling. 'Calum. Calum, they're in the house.' She squeezed her eyes against the darkness, her hands clawing at the thin coverlet.

Festus made a wild grab, attempting to wham her with the side of his Colt. Marge felt the gun pound into the bed beside her as she twisted down into the space beside the bed-frame and the wall.

A lamp was lit in a back room, and Homer Chiles – one of Judd Finch's stay-back men – was advancing on the door of Marge's bedroom.

At the same time, Calum was snapping up the barrel of his shotgun. There was little pain from his head-wound, and with his heart thumping he took a few deep breaths, thinking fast.

As Marge's door crashed open, Festus threw himself into the half-open window. As he did so, Moss panicked and fired twice into the room. The resounding noise

was terrifying, and Marge curled tight, hardly daring
to breathe.

Minch Eaves moved sideways, bringing down a
picture, the cracked glass spilling across the floor. Moss
stepped into the fragments, slipping, throwing his
hand forward.

Chiles stood dimly silhouetted by the low lamplight
behind him. He grabbed Moss's outstretched arm,
swung hard sideways. Moss's head met the doorframe
with sickening force, and as he went down Chiles
pulverized his neck with a heavy fire log. There was
early grey light against the broken window when
Chiles kicked away Moss's body. He went across the
room, then folded cruelly into the end of the bed as
Eaves's knee slammed into his ribs and the bunched
fist caught him low in the back.

Eaves could hear the gasping breaths of Marge, but
he turned away. The girl was never his business.
Getting out of the ranch house was.

He edged himself into the corridor that connected
all the other rooms. There was no sound from any part
of the house, but he knew it would only be a matter of
moments before someone from the bunkhouse made it
over. There had to be more than Chiles and the Wheat
girl. Then he remembered the injured, sick-bedded
brother, Calum.

Eaves turned to confront the movement behind him.
It was Calum standing very still, in his bare feet and
long johns. The light was deep grey, and that from the
single lamp only highlighted Calum's pale, gaunt
appearance.

Eaves confronted the shotgun in Calum's grip. He shook his head slowly as Calum's gaze bore into him.

'Tell me what you want here?' Calum said, his voice low and merciless.

'Not that it makes any difference, but it was Festus Ringwood, and he wanted your sister Marge. I think he wanted the roan, also.'

Calum nodded. 'You're right, it makes no difference, he ain't gettin' either of 'em. Where's the ugly little dandiprat now?'

'Half-way to El Paso I'd guess.'

As Eaves spoke, Marge stumbled across the floor of her bedroom. Eaves's eyes flicked to the door, then back to Calum. He made a short, fast movement with his feet, threw himself into the kitchen to one side of the corridor. He was on his knees, pulling at the outer door latch with one hand, holding a Colt revolver in the other.

'Turn around,' Calum said. 'Turn around, but don't get up.'

Eaves crabbed on his knees to face Calum. 'Why can't I get up?'

Calum pulled the trigger. 'Saves time,' he whispered bitterly, as Eaves's body lifted with the blast, splattered against the kitchen door.

Marge appeared, wavering and ghostly in the doorway behind Calum. 'You killed him,' she screamed, 'you just killed him.'

Calum dropped the shotgun at his feet, took a step towards his sister. 'Ten minutes ago there was three men in your bedroom. The walls are full of bullet holes, an' Homer's out cold. What do you think they came for, Marge? It didn't sound like you was singin' 'em a bedtime song.'

Marge shuddered, suddenly shook all over and Calum pulled her to him.

In the yard, another of Judd Finch's men was firing blindly at Festus Ringwood and Teal Markham. The Big Log men were lashing their horses away through the bend in the river, but from the bunkhouse Nate Starling was calmly hefting a .45 Springfield rifle, levering out the breech-block. As they veered through the willows, Festus was shielded by Markham, the one that had held spurs and horses for their own escape.

Nate pressed one round into the firing-chamber and pulled up on the trigger-guard. Steadying the big gun against a window frame, he could just see the dark figures move on to the range. He considered the possibility of taking out both men as he pulled the trigger.

It wasn't a clean, accurate shot, and Markham took the bullet across his chest. It was a glancing wound but, from the Springfield, enough to take a man from his saddle. Festus threw a panicked look but didn't slow, just kicked and shouted for his horse to go faster.

Half-dressed, two men raced across the river bend, throwing themselves at Markham as he rolled on the ground in agony. Ignoring the man's cries of pain, they dragged him back across the water. They held his wrists, callously forcing his head into the swirling current, then across the dirt of the yard towards the barn.

Ten minutes later, Nate was standing at the man's

feet, staring down at him. 'You're in big, big trouble, mister.'

'I just held the horses,' Markham stammered. 'That's all I came to do.'

'I'm talkin' of big trouble, if that wound ain't seen to. We can patch you up, or leave you.'

'You ain't gonna leave me like this, are you?' Markham pleaded, the pain spreading across his arms and chest.

'No, not like *that*. We'll sit you out in the sun for a few hours, give the flies an early blood-meal.'

As Nate spoke, the door to the bunkhouse flew open and the only remaining S River man burst in.

'Dee's missin',' he blurted. 'That's how they got to the house. They musta jumped 'im, spilled him in the river. There's no sign, just his gunbelt under the bridge.'

'You killed him, did you, cowboy?' Calum asked, but it wasn't really a question.

'No, it was Minch Eaves, he. . . .' The man stopped, half closed his eyes.

'That'd be about it,' Calum muttered to himself, 'I knew there was another reason for me to shoot him.' He gingerly rubbed at his temples. 'Before you make too much of a mess a the floor, I'll be askin' you to write down what you were doin' here. We'll use it as evidence against the Ringwoods. You can write, can't you?'

The man groaned, drew up his legs in suffering. 'If I do, it'll be evidence against me as well. I've got my punishment. I'm dyin'.'

Nate, laughed, cold and rough. 'I'll write it then. It's the runt we want. You just make yer mark.'

13
Approaching Law

In a room of his house in Youngsville, Judge Rowse Mallard reread the words of Calum Wheat and Nate Starling. The short note had been signed by Teal Markham.

'Hmmm, it doesn't tell us a lot. Festus Ringwood was bent on stealing a horse and maybe your sister. It indicates a culpable act, but it's not a body of evidence that would stand up in court, is it?'

Calum blurted, 'We got bodies of evidence, Judge. We dragged Dee from the Pecos, and they near done in Homer. He's another good man who'll be collectin' his pay an' moving on. You can make something of it, can't you?'

'Well, I'd like to, if for no other reason than to clear the range of carrion.' There was more than a touch of consideration in Mallard's voice. He peered at Nate and Calum. 'I'm sorry, gentlemen, but at least it reveals a motive, if and when they come at you again.

And from what you tell me, they surely will.' The judge appraised the men from S River. 'What condition is Teal Markham in?'

Nate sneered. 'He's still alive. You want one of us to bring him in?'

Mallard shook his head. 'No, no. I'll arrange for Doc Cave to ride out. I think you should keep him at the ranch. Unless you trust Wallace Suggs with his safe-keeping?'

Calum laughed. 'Yeah, we trust him all right, Judge. Trust him like a chicken trusts a pot. Acting on behalf a the people a this town, Ringwood's got himself another tame Sheriff. Yeah, we can take care a Markham.'

Judge Mallard leaned back in his chair, thought for a few seconds before responding. 'We'll get a county sheriff, I can only see this whole affair worsening. It has to end before there's any more bloodletting. These family feuds can lead to range wars. It's happened before.'

Calum railed at the speculation. 'There ain't no family feud, Judge. Ringwood wants our land. None of the S River are feudin'. So far we've only defended ourselves an' what's ours, an' that includes my brother. When him an' Budge Gourley return from El Paso, I'll pay the mortgage dues. Up to then, or when a county sheriff gets here, we'll carry on lookin' out for each other.'

Mallard raised his eyebrows at Calum's come-back. 'Why don't you both take a seat?' he suggested. 'Perhaps we can talk this through. Deliberation doesn't normally go hand in hand with the activities of this town.'

Nate started in quickly. 'How does the law get to Ringwood? He hires out his dirty work, gets them that owes him to create most a the trouble.'

Calum agreed. 'Yeah. That son of his was a mistake, though. Ringwood'll be madder'n hell when he finds out what happened at the ranch. Whatever he's after, Festus ain't improvin' his chances of gettin' it.'

Mallard held up his hand. 'Someone has to bring Barton Ringwood to heel, but it has to be the law that does it. There's elected peace officers being paid to do just that. If not a county sheriff, then I'll get a States marshal out of Roswell.'

'It's Ethan I'm worried about,' Calum said. 'Him an' Budge an' the men from Durango. They should get to El Paso all right, but then they've got to get back with the money from the sale. If anything happens to them, I ain't gonna sit back and wait for the law. An' if they ever come that near to S River again. . . .'

Nate interrupted. 'How long's it gonna take, Judge?'

'Don't honestly know, Nate. My jurisdiction only covers Santa Rosa. This could end up a state matter. I'll be in Las Cruces tomorrow. Perhaps I can get things speeded up.'

Mallard rose from his chair, extended his hand to the S River men. 'Now I have to get ready. I'm booked on the noon stage. If you'll leave this note with me, I'll get Hamming to file it in the office safe.'

Barton Ringwood was once again pacing the floor of

one of his rooms at the Boulder Hotel. The midday heat
was blistering the town. He pushed up the double
windows, ran a kerchief around his thick, clammy
neck. He slowly walked across the room, opened the
door hoping for a through breeze.

Judge Mallard's clerk was in the outside corridor,
hesitant in his approach to the rancher's suite.

'You coming to see me?' Ringwood wanted to know.
'I'd almost forgot I pay you for useful information.
Come in and earn your money.'

Tadge Hamming started talking before he'd entered
the room. 'I've got something, Mr Ringwood.'

'If it's about my son, you're wastin' my time. I
already know.'

'No, it's Wheat. Calum Wheat. He's got a note from
someone who was with Festus out at the S River.'

Ringwood blasted. 'What note? What're you talking
about?'

'I've seen it. Judge Mallard wanted it put in his safe.
It's signed by Teal Markham. Says what they went out
there to do. Says it was Festus who led 'em. He paid
'em to get the girl, Marge, an' Ethan Wheat's horse.'

'A horse?' Ringwood was bewildered.

Hamming nodded excitedly. 'Yessir, prime horseflesh
so they says. The judge is gonna keep the letter as
evidence, use it when he's ready. Judge told 'em to keep
Markham out at their place. Sounds like you're in trouble, Mr Ringwood.'

'There must be something else then?' Ringwood
goaded.

'Yes, that's what I was gettin' to. He said he'll get a

federal marshal from Roswell. An' he's seein' the state governor. Took the stage to Las Cruces about half an hour ago. Sounds like trouble all right.'

'Yes, so you keep telling me.' For a short while Ringwood considered the situation.

'You must rub with judicial proverbs, Hamming. Heard the one, "He who is a law to himself no law does need"?'

Hamming shook his head slowly. 'No sir, not put in full like that. Don't reckon it makes much sense neither, if you think about it.'

Ringwood walked across the room, turned his back to the open window. 'The sense of it is this. Someone has to rid me of Mallard.'

Hamming took a step back, held up his hands. 'You only pay me for information, Mr Ringwood. What you do, or make of it, is up to you.'

Ringwood's face darkened. 'You can serve time for what you've already done today, Hamming. There's only one way I could have come by the information I've got. If anything happens to me because of it, your future ain't worth a plugged nickel. Think about it. We both need Mallard out of the way.'

Hamming clasped his hands in front of him. 'Just supposin' ... if I went along with ... what's to be done?' he faltered.

Ringwood's eyes flashed. 'He's taking the stage to Las Cruces? Well, there's a stop at Piñon. Not Orogrande, that's a relay station, too busy. Piñon, that's where you can do it.'

'Do what?'

'Kill him. You shoot him, Tadge.'

'You expect me to shoot a man in cold blood? A judge?'

'Don't look upon him as a judge. See him as a man who's out to stop you gettin' on in the world.' Ringwood grinned encouragingly at young Hamming. 'I'll take care of everything, Tadge. Just get it done.'

Without taking his eyes off Hamming, Ringwood sorted out a wad of folding money. 'From now on, I'll be needing some help with papers, legal documents and the like. Say five hundred dollars to get you started. Call it your first pay-day from Big Log.'

Hamming chewed on his bottom lip. 'That's more than I'd make in a long time stuck with Mallard. But I'll need a gun, and a horse. One that runs.'

'Go to the livery stable. Tell Betts you're working for me. He'll sort you a good mount. Ask him for a shotgun. That'll be best for what you've got to do. At Piñon, don't talk to Mallard. Get up close. Shoot him, then get out, fast. You understand?'

Hamming nodded. 'You'll protect me? Federal law won't overlook the killing of a county judge.'

Ringwood drew a bottle of his favoured bourbon from a cabinet. He poured some into two large glasses, handed one to the clerk. 'It's early, but we'll drink to the fact that, right now, there's no law for you to worry about.'

An hour later, Hamming was riding south to meet the stage at Piñon.

14
River Camp

Throughout the hottest part of the day, the S River men pushed the cattle. Weary and rueful, Ethan sat the roan and watched. Mid-afternoon, he decided to move them up. He had to try again for water in the higher ground.

Their small chuck-and-water wagon kept to the flats, but the herd spread out on a shoal to the higher ground, sniffing the rocks and bawling for water. Eventually they found a stale, dried-out creek, but the men didn't make much of a fuss. They started crowding the cattle, winding them in and out along the stream bed towards a place where they hoped there'd be puddle water.

For another couple of hours they staggered towards Hueco. Judd Finch and Budge watched the lead steers as they scuttled through the shaled pass, watched anxiously as the cries and bellows of the cattle grew.

After a while the roughness of the ground softened

and they rode into a landscape devoid of edge or focus. The bare earth held only enough moisture to support patches of creosote and scrub-grass, but it was enough. The cattle sensed water scratches, then broke into an eye-bulging, free run.

They were into Blanca Flats, where small underground springs occasionally pocked the barren ground. There was no need to contain the herd, they were all headed for the first drink.

The shallow spring guttered across the hot warm earth, but it was clean. There was little movement in the watercourse, just enough to prevent the miasma of illness or death. The men dismounted, relief etched into their seared faces.

Ethan hesitated as they led the eager mounts forward. Budge eyed him, winked thoughtfully, recognizing the doubt as hundreds of mouths pressed for the water.

After the first long pull, the horses raised their dripping jowls, one after another. They snorted, sloped their necks and drank again.

Ethan wished the Tahl-Tan could have held on a bit longer, been a bit brighter. He turned to Budge. 'When me an' Cal was kids, we thought drivin' a herd a longhorns to the border was a trail to paradise. I wouldn't give you pennies for it now.'

Judge Rowse Mallard sat alone at a bench in the waiting-room of the Piñon staging-post. Reading a back copy of the *Santa Rosa Gazette*, he toyed with a mug of cold, stewed coffee. Outside, there was the chink of chain and the snap of leather; the stage driver was making a play of checking the traces in readiness for the second leg of the journey to Las Cruces.

The judge had delayed for nearly an hour. He was going to wait a bit longer, but the driver was restless to get moving again. Then suddenly, as he folded the newspaper, his nerves tightened when a shadow fell across the dust-blown floor.

In the rear doorway, Tadge Hamming cocked the hammers of his shotgun. He'd ridden in from the south unseen, screened by the logged walls of the staging-post. He swung up the twin barrels to face Mallard, but didn't speak.

The judge twitched at the deadly, ominous sound. He'd been ready for it, but the reality was none the less a shock. 'If you're going to shoot me, at least come in and do it,' he said unsurely.

Hamming took one step forward, less than ten feet from where the judge sat.

Mallard twisted slowly in his chair. 'My own clerk,' he said, staring at Hamming. 'What a disappointment. For a while I've been wondering just how Barton Ringwood could be so well apprised of my office. I didn't think it would be you who'd turn up here, Tadge, but with that information I gave you, it was a fair guess somebody would.'

Hamming brandished the shotgun. 'If you knew that, Judge, you don't appear to have set yourself up too good.'

There was a sharp, hostile cut to the judge's voice. 'That's why there's no one else on the stage. Couldn't have anyone getting hurt on my account, could we?'

'What you talking about?' Hamming gaped.

'The stage-driver's name is Farr Jawkin, and he's standing where you were a minute ago. Looks to me like he's holding a small cannon, and it's only inches from where your brain's been hiding.'

Hamming felt the jolt of steel at the base of his spine. He trembled as he recalled Ringwood's futile advice. The words rang around the bleak interior of the room. *Don't talk . . . shoot him . . . get out fast.*

'Drop the gun, sonny,' Jawkin murmured across Hamming's shoulder. 'First let them hammers down easy.'

Hamming did as he was told. 'What's going to happen now?' he asked, his voice cracking with uncertainty.

'Youngsville will get an honest peace officer, and hopefully the legal back-up that goes with it. What have *you* gained from this, Tadge, other than a few years behind bars?'

Uninterested in an explanation or come-back, Mallard rose from the bench. He looked severely at the stage-driver. 'He can ride with you, Farr. He'll be no trouble, and he won't be going anywhere until we get to Las Cruces.'

Jawkin gritted. 'Shame. What this godforsaken place needs is a big, soft red carpet spread across the floor.'

The judge stepped out into the evening, adjusted his hat. 'There'll soon be Ringwood men held right across the state. If anyone wants a job, it'll be full time riding the bilbo wagon.'

*

The following day, the S River herd moved on towards the Rio Grande. For twenty miles they walked for the crossing near Berino. Beyond there, grassland led to the pens of El Paso.

Ethan wasn't sure of how long Calum had reckoned for the drive, but he remembered him saying to put some lard on the beeves. They could ease up, use the grass for at least another day.

During late afternoon, the provision wagon rolled into camp. It was welcome relief for those who'd already begun to worry about another cold, makeshift meal.

At first dark, while the men hooted for their beans and bacon, Ethan was telling Budge of his plans for the next few days.

'We'll play down our arrival, in case there's anyone from Big Log waiting. There's good ground ahead, Budge. We're still off where the main trails come in, an' we can take our time. Once we reach the river, I'll ride into town alone.'

Budge looked surprised, unsure. 'That don't sound like a great idea. Your brother told me the best way to keep outa trouble is by not gettin' into it.'

Ethan shrugged. 'He never told me that. But he told me what to do in El Paso. The buyer's name is Barston. I'll bring him out to survey the herd an' make a cash deal. You an' the boys can then hightail it back to the ranch. Calum'll want to make payment in Youngsville. Once the mortgage's paid up, Ringwood'll have to point his guns in another direction.'

15
The Cattle Deal

By the time Ethan was ready to start his journey into
El Paso, a clear orange glow was spreading up from the
eastern horizon. The morning air was filled with fresh
stimulating fragrances. Some drifted in from the baked
surfaces of the red earth, some from the tree-blossom
and basket-grasses that lined the banks of the Rio
Grande. But there were other feral scents that drifted
from the cow town. It was those that the roan tested
uneasily for some time before returning to play with
his rig and empty oat-sack.

Ethan called him and he came half-way over, still
chewing on the crumpled remains of the feed-bag. He
tossed it high in the air, snorted loudly and whammed
it with a front hoof. He stopped ostentatiously and held
up his head for approval. He was eager and ready.
Within ten minutes Ethan had him loosely snaffled
and ready to move out.

They faced the expanse ahead of them, watching the
land take shape in the early light. They would make

town by midday. Ethan raised a hand to Budge, nodded at Judd who was watching the herd. He mounted and eased the horse gently forward through the graze.

Ethan rode into the southern end of El Paso. He avoided the middle of town where end-of-trail cowboys spilled from the flop-houses and cheap saloon bars. The roan roused some interest as Ethan looked for the Cattlemen's Association, but everyone appeared more interested in spreading their own play.

The building he was looking for sat wedged between a hardware store and a photographer's studio. There was a picture display of scrubbed drovers propped self-conscious in linsey-woolsey suits, derbys and fancy shirts.

A man outside the hardware store looked up as Ethan dismounted, stared unwelcomingly as he broomed out the range dirt.

Ethan tethered the roan close to the door of the cattlemen's office. He pushed the back of his hand up to the horse's nose. 'I don't like it either, but what can we do? I'll make it short,' he said, looking up and down the street.

'I'm lookin' for Mr Sam Barston,' Ethan told one of two men who sat at facing desks. The large room smelled of pine, old ledgers and paper.

'That's me,' said the man Ethan had spoken to. 'You look like you're off the trail. Cattle to sell, is it?'

'Yeah, 'bout three hundred head. Mostly longhorn. They're bedded down across the river. I want to keep 'em there.'

Barston looked keenly at Ethan, then nodded. 'Keep 'em feedin'. Not such a bad idea.'

Ethan agreed. It wasn't totally what he had in mind, but it was prudent. 'Can you ride out with me?' he asked. 'Shouldn't take more'n a couple of hours.'

Barston looked at his colleague for confirmation. 'There's a big herd from Hachita comin' in tomorrow. Sounds like I'll be needin' the rest of today.'

'Can you bring cash? There's reasons why, an' I'm prepared to take a drop in price 'cause of it.' Ethan looked suitably open.

Barston grinned. 'You want cash, an' I've got to get myself half-cooked for the pleasure of it. You'll be takin' a drop in price all right, son.'

Ethan kicked his heels, looked out at the roan as Barston considered how much to take from the association safe. The buyer pulled on a sugarloaf hat and estimated Ethan. 'It's a fair amount a money I'm carryin', cowboy,' he said. 'I hope you'll be lookin' out for me?'

As they stepped on to the boardwalk, Ethan answered. 'If anything happens to you, Mr Barston, I'll make sure the money gets to where it's goin'.'

Barston chuckled. 'I'm sure you will, son, I'm sure you will. Let's get outa this cow town.'

It was when Barston swung his rig around in front of the cattlemen's office that Doughy Seaton caught sight of Ethan.

Ethan was pulling himself into the saddle as the Big Log rider was crossing the street from one saloon to another.

Seaton turned quickly into a side alley, watched furtively as the two men rode out of town. He saw them head west, saw the chance of making more dollars from Festus.

Alongside the Rio Grande, Ethan reined in as Sam Barston pulled his rig up to the wide, shallow crossing.

'You can smell 'em. We'll spot 'em from the far bank. They'll be two or three miles beyond, where my boys are holdin' 'em,' Ethan said.

As he faced Barston, Ethan saw a movement in the distance. It was only a blemish, but against the flatness of the range there was no doubt it was a mounted rider. As Ethan watched, it became a motionless shimmering speck. Someone was holding off about two miles back.

Barston caught Ethan's gaze. 'What you seen?'

Ethan tugged at the brim of his Stetson. 'A rider. He musta been trailin' us from El Paso.'

How do you know he's trailin' us?'

' 'Cause he ain't comin' any closer. It's sorta what I been expectin'.'

As the men turned into the running water, Barston looked across at Ethan. 'Who is he?' he called.

'I'm guessin' it's a friend of a friend, Mr Barston. All the way from Santa Rosa. I've got somethin' someone else wants.'

Barston flicked out anxiously at his rig horse. 'I bet I'm carryin' the somethin'.'

'The sooner we make the deal, the sooner you'll be safe. If it's who I think it is, it's the money they're after. They won't be interested in the cattle any more.'

It took less than an hour for Barston to make a general survey of the herd and make payment. As Calum had told Ethan, it was below market price, but in the circumstances, Ethan considered $3,000 to be fair.

'You gonna guarantee my safety back to town, son?' Barston was looking east, back towards El Paso.

'I told you. It's the money they're after. You've got through the scary bit. The boys'll be ridin' back home with that parcel a cash.'

Barston was still worried. 'Who'll be lookin' after the herd I've just bought?'

'They won't go beyond the river. The night'll bring 'em home. Send your stockmen out tomorrow.'

Barston shoved a fat cigar into his mouth, gripped it firmly between his teeth. 'As you say, them beeves're goin' nowhere. I'll send for 'em when you an' your friends are well gone.'

As the cattle-buyer rolled his rig across the Rio Grande, Budge threw Ethan a puzzled look. 'What was that about ridin' back home? You're not comin' with us?'

'Not right off, Budge. I'm the poorer for one or two store-boughts. I'll be right behind you though. A rear-guard might not be a bad idea.'

'Yeah. I think you're right about what Ringwood's up to. You just take care. I don't want to have to explain anythin' real bad to your kin.'

Ethan turned to Judd Finch. 'Judd, you an' your men ride wide. Watch the horizon. There ain't no one friendly out here.'

Judd grinned, patted his Colt. 'That's what we're here for Ethan. You do the same. How long you stayin'?'

'Until tomorrow. For tonight, I'll spread a blanket among a few hundred longhorns.'

For the second time that day, Ethan ended the farewells. He stood patting the roan's heavy neck as Budge and Judd and his men swung north-east, towards the salt flats.

'We'll see you back at the ranch.' Judd waved his hat.

'If you're more'n a full day behind, we'll come lookin' for you,' Budge shouted.

Ethan walked the roan along the shallows. With his few remaining dollars, the next meal for both of them would be store-bought. Bran mash, pony nuts and hay, maybe a carrot or two and a big green apple. For Ethan something with spices and pastry baked in an oven, a dish of vegetables and anything covered with sugar and cream. All of it served on patterned china.

15
Horse Dealing

At the same time as Sam Barston was closing down for the night, a few diehard customers of Fat Jack's sat with their whiskey and cards. The saloon only had two small windows at the front, but a few boney candles were burning. Against the near wall, an old man with a beaver hat let the front legs of his chair clack to the floor. He was still fast asleep, but it aroused the attention of three men who were sitting at a nearby table.

After his narrow escape from S River ranch, Festus Ringwood had caught up with Doughy Seaton and Little Copper. Dutch Joe and two other hands had already left town. They'd crossed the Rio Grande, on their way to Sonora. There'd be nothing for them back in Youngsville. In their failure to knock the S River herd, Big Log with Barton Ringwood would be a bleak and dangerous place.

Rafer Tymes was still alive, and wanted to make his money. He knew there'd be no way of catching the S

River men. With their cattle-money, they'd be making a fast ride back to Santa Rosa. There'd have to be another time and place for him to collect his $2,000.

Seaton threw a wily glance at Little Copper. 'I ain't seen a dollar since we left Big Log. The whores a this town only give *so* much on a handshake.'

Festus leaned in close. 'You'll get paid when we get back to the ranch.' He grinned. 'An' my ol' man gave you a good mount, don't forget.'

Little Copper raised his glass towards Festus, and for a moment or two they choked on lewd noises.

Seaton was still unhappy. 'I needn't a told you what I saw earlier on. You owe me for that. I coulda got shot if Wheat had seen me. No sir, I'm thinkin' a movin' on. Arizona, California, maybe. I hear it's rich out there, plenty a pickin's.'

Festus just eyed him, thoughtfully.

Seaton looked up as a drunk shouted, 'Get a tune outa that pianner.' The lone barman walked across the room and slammed his fingers across the stained, beaten keys.

Little Copper leered. 'If we rode west, Doughy, you wouldn't have much chance with them rich pickin's you're so fond of.' He winked slyly. 'Not once they'd had a good close look at me.'

Seaton looked restless, unsure. 'What you got in mind, Festus? I don't wanna hang around here with no prospects.'

Festus leaned in close to Doughy. 'We all missed out on the herd, yeah. But it's the sellin' money that's important. They'll be ridin' back now. All we gotta do is dog 'em. In the meantime, why not help me get to Wheat? Get under his skin. Jiggle his rope.'

Doughy tipped his bottle. 'How you gonna do that, Festus? Stick out yer tongue? Stand in the middle of the street callin' him names. You know you ain't goin' up against him with a gun.'

'Yeah, that's up to Rafer Tymes. He's playin' the longer game now, I was thinkin' more of a short diversion.'

At the mention of Tymes, Seaton cast a quick distracted look around the bar. 'Anyone seen that gunny lately?'

Festus made a shallow smile. No,' he said. 'He ain't one for time wastin'. He knows he's the one Wheat has to take care of. He'll ride back to Santa Rosa, an' Wheat'll follow.'

Little Copper tossed his head back, drained his glass. 'I hope that diversion's not one where me an' Doughy gets blown to pieces.'

Festus shook his head, slowly. 'No. I bin' thinkin' more indirect. It's gonna be somethin' different. Somethin' personal. Somethin' that'll give us a chaff, alongsides.'

Little Copper and Doughy shared a doubtful glance. 'Why, Festus?' Doughy asked.

Festus looked hard at his fingers gripped tight around his empty glass. 'Just because,' he snapped, banging his fist on the table.

The two men nodded indulgently at the spoiled son of a rich, venal rancher.

'Tell us about it,' Little Copper said. Then he

shouted across at the piano player. 'Leave that. Get some food and more light in this place.'

The three men never came closer than a half mile during the early morning dark. Ethan had heard nothing, and even if he had, from that distance they could have shot him as he clambered from his blanket, before he got to his guns. He could see them plainly, colourless, but definite against the low sun. They'd brought an oestrus mare, the only enticement his roan would respond to.

It would have caught an enchanting drift on the light westerly breeze, and from that distance would have wandered off on an interested walk. But within 200 yards the stallion would have a clear sighting, and its senses would be fully aroused. There was no faith or whistling potent enough to compete with that primal instinct.

They rode away in single file, with the mare and stallion in the rear. Leading at a trot was Festus Ringwood. Little Copper and Doughy Seaton were trailing in line with a lead on the horses.

With the Spencer Ethan could have dropped all three, but they'd considered that, and presented him with a narrow target protected by his precious stallion.

He watched them for nearly an hour, until the first heat-shimmer rose to envelop them; then all that remained was a few dark specks sinking in a surface of rippling grassland.

To Ethan it looked like they wanted to draw him across the river back to El Paso, or for him to die in the attempt. Either way, it was wretched entertainment.

In a straight line, the town was more than twenty miles distant. By day and on foot, the range would turn to a searing hot-plate. The journey was unthinkable in less than two days. He could wait for Barston's stockmen or travel by night, but that held its own primitive fears. Ethan had no choice. He'd take his guns, saddle pouch and water-skin, and a grinding capacity for revenge.

17
The Roan Fights

With Seaton leading the oestrus mare, Festus coaxed the roan towards one of the cracked barns that edged the southern end of the town.

Burlap awnings on the cratewood shanties hung wearily in the hot, still air. A lank-haired cowboy staggered from beneath a hackberry bush and shook a bottle tauntingly at Festus as he passed. A girl so thin her clothes had fallen off, stared with naked despair. A *niño* tyke rose from a dirt pile and stared wide-eyed; not so much at Festus, but at the big, gleaming roan being led to its reckoning.

In a corral at the open end of the barn Little Copper held in a dun-coloured mustang. It was untried, desperate with the torment of capture. It was going to be a test, the sort of encounter that revealed the ugly slant to Festus Ringwood.

Festus tugged at the rope halter around the roan's neck. Ethan's stallion saw the wild horse immediately, and in his uncertainty and unfamiliar surroundings, rubbed in close to the logged bars of the corral. He turned his head from sideways on, alarmed and defensive. The dun snorted aggressively, and stamped towards the inevitable attack. It came on, but the roan didn't shy away. Instead he moved forward, his steps light and cautious.

The stallions swung their faces in close, overlapping until their jowls were almost touching. Deliberately, the dun lowered its great bony head. It was a slow movement, dire and threatening, but the roan didn't argue with the challenge. The stallions wove powerful arcs with their necks, cutting and thrusting, until the head of each horse was probing between the forefeet of his opponent. They were set in their efforts to get lower, and they pressed until their flaring nostrils were within a few inches of the ground.

They sucked in great draughts of air until their necks were corded and swollen. Their chests bulged with anticipation, and for a while they remained still, their muscles tightly sprung and shimmering in the morning light. It was the silence of impending combat, and nothing moved, only their fleshy nostrils which blew violent squalls of dust across the pummelled ground. Each horse was seeking leverage and supremacy, sensing and waiting for a sign of weakness. It ended suddenly when the dun squealed and whirled in a complete circle, twisting its hindquarter and lashing out with its massive hooves.

The preliminaries were over, and from fifteen feet the dun rose on its cannons and advanced like a fistfighter intending to smash its way ahead.

Its flailing forelegs pounded the air head-on to the roan, but the stallion railed from the bone-crushing attack and swung round to thrash his own rear hooves low at the enraged mustang. There was one glancing strike, but it caught the dun in the ribs and drew a sharp bellow. It dropped to all-fours and whirled to face the roan. There was a shuddering rage in its scream, and it sprayed fountains of saliva high across the pen. The roan was driving it to more frustration, and the dun pounded the ground in fury.

With its jaws spread, and the cutting edges of its great molars bared, the dun rushed, but the roan wasn't there. He'd leaped from the punishing teeth that could snap a leg-bone as if it was a bar of candy. He'd moved out of range, tempting and very dangerous. The dun's rage carried it into one angry bellowing charge after another, its shoulders heaved and sweat darkened its jugular run.

The roan was presenting one opportunity after another, but was evading each attack by muscle and swerve, driving the big dun into a fury of bewilderment and disorientation. There was an inevitable open moment when it lagged in turning round, and both of the roan's hind feet landed solidly against its ribs. The dun grunted with pain, and its great strength suddenly faltered into signs of uncertainty. It came to a halt, and stood in the centre of the pen glaring belligerently at its elusive opponent. Its flanks were heaving from the exertion, and rivers of sweat were dripping from its belly.

The roan sensed victory and pranced tantalizingly close. There was no response from the dun, and it veered from the onslaught. It tried to move away, but the roan swung around in front barring its progress, edging a half-step forward, springing his heels in a sharp gesture.

The *niño* heard the murderous whinnies piercing the air. His skin tingled, and he sprang to his feet. He understood the noise, and ran wildly. He slithered under the raised floor of a cabin, brought himself to the outer poles of the corral. The sight before him was terrifying.

Both stallions stood very still. They flexed and panted, their bodies heaving against the pen-rails and the flats beyond. A few seconds passed while they measured each other for gesture and nerve, then the roan whirled and flew into another attack. The dun was surprised by the quickness of the move, and then the roan was above it, towering on his hind legs and driving with punching forefeet. The dun started in retreat, backing away confused, but not before a cruel blow slashed into one of its ears. The roan chased his advantage, balancing on his hind feet, using his fore-hoofs like fists. The dun emitted an enraged scream and abandoned its attempt to break away. Using brute strength, it came up through the driving whirl of its opponent's hoofs, taking blows on its neck and chest to settle a face-off with the roan.

The dun was half blinded by the blood that cascaded across the side of its head from the torn ear, but it seemed oblivious to pain and the blows it was receiving. It struck out with its huge bony hoofs in desperate frenzy, and the roan threw out his head in an attempt to seize one of the punishing forelegs. But before the roan realized it, a powerful gnash raked down his neck and ripped out a great wad of hair and outer hide.

The roan went down on his knees, but kept his balance. He thrust himself up, and in the same instant caught the dun squarely on the chest with his driving hind feet. The dun retaliated with another seizure from its jaws. It opened two deep gashes in the roan's hip, and blood welled across the sweat-stained buttock.

Across the corral, the *niño* could see Festus had been joined by more men. They were laughing and joshing, some of their words pierced the fearful noise. 'No one'll ride him after this. He's going back to the wild. Ten dollars says he'll kill the dun.'

They tossed coin and folding-money at each other's feet, making wagers on the outcome of the fight.

The dun came to a halt on spraddled legs and stood there, exhausted and blinded. Sweat dripped from its body, and blood trickled in thin streams across its muzzle. Dimly it saw the roan coming back to the attack, and gamely it reared and struck. But its feet found only thin air. A succession of blows was rained against its right shoulder, thudding in a blanket of foaming sweat. The blows then came from the left side, landing high on its withers. It threw its weight into the roan, seeking to knock him down, but the stallion whirled and landed on all fours. He lashed out his hind feet, and one of them caught the dun on the lower jaw. The great hoof pounded through soft flesh, and crushed teeth and bone. The dun turned, reared once and charged. It took great strides, thrusting madly at the air, hooking and scything with its front hoofs, but the roan skidded away. The dun dropped back to earth and turned to face its adversary, but its movements were exhausted and clumsy.

Festus and the men with him grabbed at the money in front of them. They made vehement noises as they moved off, shoving each other, kicking and spitting at the ground. The *niño* watched, mesmerized. He pulled himself on to his bony elbows, dragged himself to a broken water trough that abutted the corral, flung his senses back to the horses.

The mustang was beaten and knew it. Its strength was gone and the power and quickness had flown from its legs. There was no escape, and it stood and defended himself as best it could. It tried to locate its adversary through the bloody mist, dodging and parrying, occasionally giving ground, but still dogged and reluctant. The roan returned to the attack, lashing without mercy. Drenched with blood and sweat, he went about the task of beating his opponent to the earth. But the dun was hard, and took the blows, even after it had ceased to defend. It was a mass of bruises, cuts and gashes, and its jaw hung cruel and broken. It stood with its four legs spread, and braced itself, anger and defiance still in its heart. But at last as the night descended, its big bony knees buckled and it slid slowly to the damp scarred earth. The mustang turned on its side and crooked its neck, a great sigh came heavy and full-flecked from its nostrils.

The roan raised his head which gleamed hard and lustrous under the rising sun.

The *niño* was awe-struck. The air was oppressive and filled with raw sensations. His heart was pounding; it hurt, and he buried his small, callow face in the crook of his arm.

18
Under the Sun

Ethan sat cross-legged, pulled his traps towards him. He drew the Remington and cocked it, letting the hammer down on the half-cock notch. He turned the cylinder and looked at the caps and chambers. He full-cocked the hammer, then eased it forward with his thumb. Then he eased himself on to his knees and peered east.

The air became warmer, and the sky was turning light blue, free from cloud. The long, spare shadows of the early hours withdrew across the land as the sun broke from a shoulder of the distant Sacramentos. He shielded his eyes with his hand and savagely contemplated the stretch back to El Paso. Within a few feet, grasshoppers flicked their legs. In seconds, they buried themselves in the rootgrass, seeking shelter from the hostility of the day.

Ethan wrapped the loops of the saddle pouch around the long barrel of the Spencer. Gripping the breech, he set himself towards the town.

As the sun rose higher, hunger gnawed. He found some wild onions and started a fire the Indian way with dry splinters. He improvised with long-john fluff and brush. The onions were small but moist, and with liquorice-fern and a handful of plump grasshoppers he roasted a meagre but tasty meal.

After a few hours, Ethan's appearance was raw and distressing. His sinews were knotted, his legs ached. As the morning opened up, a shudder of presentiment racked his body. The purpose of his return bit into him.

It was rapidly approaching midday when he found what he was looking for. It was a long wedge of dry mud that shelved into the ground. There was low shelter beneath it, and from noon it would be refuge from the burning slant of the sun. He eased himself into the narrow cleft, pushing his traps tightly in behind him.

He stretched out his arm and ran his fingers around a dried imprint, one of many that circled the edge of the mound. Even with iron shoes, Ethan knew the hoof print. It was as moving and unforgettable as it had been in the foothills of the Sangre de Christos where he'd tracked and won the roan.

The sun was at its fiercest and its heat beat up from the ground. The silence and isolation created the void he needed and within five minutes he drifted into an abyss of sleep.

Ethan was aware of the musty, animal tang as he woke from his darkness.

He stared up into the face of a human buffalo, instinctively groped behind him for his Colt. But the apparition grunted from deep in his throat, forced the barrel end of the Spencer down into Ethan's shoulder.

'You're in no shape to try that,' the mountain man growled at him. 'If I'd wanted to skin you, I could've done it anytime since noon.'

Ethan had slept semi-deliriously for almost four hours. He blinked against the dipping sun, painfully eased himself to his knees. He looked around him, saw two sway-back mules standing twenty feet away, nosing a patch of mesquite.

'I can only guess at which way you're headed, but the mess you're in, you'll never get there. I'd have put you down for a dead'un all right.' The man spat a thin stream of dark juice over his shoulder and took a step back.

Ethan climbed stiffly to his feet. 'Where'd you come from?'

The mountain man hawked into the mesquite. 'Here and there. Now and then I supply critters to the livery. I'm just wonderin' to meself, what they'd pay for you.'

Ethan stood unprotected and vulnerable, rubbing his hands together. 'You're going to El Paso?'

'Them's me mules yonder. Can you see any other critters? Wake up, dope. El Paso is where I'm *from*.'

Ethan stared around him at the desolate rangeland. 'Well, you ain't much use to me then. Just give me back my gun and point me in the right direction.'

'You'll need that sense of reality, mister, if you're goin' there. 'Specially in that condition. Most of 'em look like you when they've come away.' The mountain man squinted and looked Ethan up and down.

Ethan squinted back at him. 'These are my working clothes, and I've had a bit a trouble gettin' here,' he said. 'I've got a horse to collect and something of a debt to settle.'

A deep, chesty laugh erupted from the mountain man. 'So that's what you're doing out here, lookin' fer some horse thieves. I'll wager yer debt's for more than that. But I reckon that's none a' my business.'

Ben rubbed the back of his neck and attempted a spit. 'That's right, it's strictly personal. What do you know of my horse? You've seen the roan?'

The mountain man yanked at his greasy skin trousers. 'Ain't *seen*. Heard tell of. A blood like that, had to belong to somebody with a touch a colour.'

He looked closely into Ethan's eyes. 'Don't let revenge get ahead of you, son. Wait 'til you're ready. No sense you goin' to hell jus' 'cause somebody else is.'

Ethan turned his head sideways-on to the the old trapper. 'I don't want to seem ungrateful, but what's it matter to you?'

' 'Cos I heard summat this mornin'. Summat about the scum that took yer horse.' The mountain man nodded obligingly and held out Ethan's carbine. 'They won't waste any time in gettin' long gone. They were trash, cowardly rabble.'

The old man spat another stream of juice then walked over to his mules to untie a sack of provisions. 'Heard tell, the big roan's in a corral at the south end a town. A place that ain't fit for man nor beast.'

It was night time, and Ethan was within a quarter

mile of El Paso. A few hours earlier, the old mountain man had helped him collect his thoughts and prepare.

Riding one of the mules, he made a cautious advance on the town's broken ribbons of light. He dismounted, pulled down his Spencer and canvas pouch, watched the mule turn back to the mountain man.

The moon was early in its first quarter, and the sky was turning from deep grey to black. He turned to the short, furrowed alleys, and moved warily until he reached the spine of the main street. He edged his way further south, along the backs of the shanties towards the corral.

The *niño* was sitting by the dirt pile. He looked up, gripped himself as he watched the man who'd come for the big, brave horse. He followed closely in the deep shadows, wanted to see them meet up.

The roan stood ready and alert, listening for any sign of approach. Ethan found the corral in the increasing darkness and blew a short, low whistle. The beaten mustang was gone, and the stallion tossed its head at Ethan's nearness. Ethan reached for the rope halter around its neck, made soothing noises as he kicked out the corral bars. He held the stallion's head down close, led it further away from its cruel circus.

Beyond the tents and flop-houses he found a shack big enough to shelter them. It was well removed and hidden from the main street and buildings of the town. Ethan had to get to the livery stable, then find a few provisions, make sure the stallion was secure. For reassurance he draped his skin coat around its neck, saw the wounds, the dark open gashes in the gleaming rump.

As he set out for the livery stable he stepped across a broken pulpit board. In the darkness the words were just visible. TODAY'S MOLEHILLS ARE TOMORROW'S MOUNTAINS. 'Musta been a cattle rancher,' he mumbled.

The blacksmith was sitting in the workshop annexed to the stable. There was a lamp still burning and Ethan tapped the open door with his foot. He spoke softly.

'I know it's late and you're probably real tired, but I need your help.'

The blacksmith didn't look up, just grunted out a reply. 'Too late an' too damn tired. Come back in the mornin'.'

Ethan smiled and walked forward, kicked the chair out from under the sullen feller. 'Sorry, but I don't reckon that'd make much sense to my injured horse, mister.'

The blacksmith scrambled to his feet, reaching for a pick-hammer. 'This'll make sense, dirt-bag. Come bustin' in here. I'll . . .'

In one fast movement, Ethan drew his Bowie knife and hacked down into the long shaft of the hammer. 'I don't want to damage *you* yet, you've got some work to do. Get your fire drawn up, now. In twenty minutes you're gonna shoe me a horse. An' find me a needle, some thread, and a bottle of alcohol. I'll also need a saddle.'

The blacksmith understood, quickly saw the point of Ethan's argument; he reached a heavy hand to the bellows.

Ethan watched as the fire produced a small, rekindled glow. He nodded unpleasantly. 'When I return, if there's anyone here but you, think on this. You won't be makin' much of a livin' without arms.'

The men's eyes met in silent understanding. Ethan pushed his big knife back into his waistband and turned away, undoubted.

A short while later, while the roan was being shod, Ethan cleaned and sewed the rump wound. He told the blacksmith to mark up the cost of a thirty-dollar saddle, a saddle blanket and a bag of oats to Barton Ringwood.

Ethan led the roan into the darkened street, listened for a moment to the town's bawdy, eager amusement. It wasn't as he'd planned, but forgoing a table meal was a tad less wholesome than an immediate return to Santa Rosa.

From his dirt pile, the *niño* watched as the dark shadowy figure of Ethan cantered quietly out of El Paso. He banged his fists happily against his knees and grinned. When the old mountain man returned in a few weeks, he'd tell him what he'd seen. Maybe get another rattler's tail for bein' a good watcher.

The S River herd were aware of the rider as they stood chewing. They looked up, puffed unconcerned and lowered their heads again. Ethan passed on, looped to the east, rode slowly towards the rim of the salt flats. He faced a cool northerly breeze, saw the big headlight of the night train still ten miles off El Paso. The grass along the Rio Grande gradually broke to poorer ground. The roan dipped its head, seemed doubtful of the route and looked back to the west. Ethan gently heeled him on. 'Your memory ain't too good, is it,' he said.

19
County Law

County Sheriff Giles Woodman listened attentively to Judge Mallard. The Las Cruces lawman wore a town suit. He was slim built and carried thick, heavy moustachios. He was a young man, but shrewd and exacting. He was known for his intolerance of backsliders and harmful crime, could turn a blind eye to the petty offences of erstwhile law-abiders.

'Well, you've stacked a convincing hand against this Barton Ringwood, Judge. A lot depends on those witnesses, but if they can make court, and you can tie in that attack on the ranch, you should have him. I'm no expert on the law, that's your territory.'

'But enforcing it's yours, Sheriff.' Mallard looked around the office, at the glass-fronted gun case that held Winchester rifles and shotguns. 'I already have one statement, and Lamming's will indict Ringwood. You think there's a problem with that?'

'Ringwood could be your problem. He's no greenhorn. From what you say, he carries a lot of muscle in your town. When he finds out – and he certainly will – that there's evidence enough to put him in a state penitentiary, he won't roll over. He'll use that muscle.'

'To do what?'

'You know as well as I do, Judge. He'll try bribing, and if he has to, he'll kill them. He's a lot to lose.'

Mallard was visibly worried, nervous. 'If he succeeds, not only do the Wheats go down, but the town'll be back to where it started.'

Woodman jerked his head toward the street. 'Ever thought of moving to Las Cruces, Judge?'

'There was a time not so long ago when I'd have walked away. But it's a good little town, Sheriff. Or was before the likes of Ringwood. It will be again before long, and it can grow. It needs a timely, legal purge.'

'Yep. I believe you. But men like Ringwood have power. A lot of people believe that squares up with right. That bothers me.'

'How can he do anything as long as Hamming and Markham are held safe?'

Woodman pulled at his moustachios, looked keenly at Mallard. 'Well, Hamming's safe enough, but Markham? For all we know, Ringwood could be filling his plot as we speak. And let's not forget that juries can be worked on, Judge.'

Mallard got to his feet. 'For God's sake, man, you sound beat before you've started. Sure all that might happen, but it's your job to try and stop such things. What was this reputation of yours built on?'

Woodman held up a restraining hand. 'Whoa. I'm

just covering the ground. I'm coming back to Youngsville with you. Always was. From what I've learned of your 'good little town', I wanted to see which way you set sail.'

'Into the wind, Sheriff,' Mallard retorted. 'You'll be bringing someone with you?' he asked.

Woodman half smiled. 'I'll be bringing a deputy. Chud Barker. He'll take up his position immediately. The present office-holder, what's his name . . . Suggs? He hasn't been there long enough to draw a month's pay, let alone a pension. Barker'll clear him out, then deputize as he thinks fit. In the meanwhile I'll speak to Markham and Hamming. Is there anything I might have overlooked?'

'Not that I can think of. We can go back with Hamming. Take the night stage.'

'Yes, Judge. Meet me back here at seven-thirty.'

Mallard crossed Main Street from the sheriff's office to one of the town's three hotels. He had small judicial matters to attend to, but before that he needed a decent meal and time for reflection.

Woodman had officially requisitioned the night stage into Santa Rosa. There were no stops, other than a detour to S River ranch to take Teal Markham from the unpredictable charge of Nate Starling and Calum Wheat.

With both Ringwood's henchmen on board, the stage reached Youngsville shortly before first light.

As his last official duty, Wallace Suggs was ordered to supply food and bang up the prisoners. Out of the habit of such crude surroundings, Giles Woodman kept his questioning of the two men to less than an hour.

In the rank, sweaty confines of the jail, Hamming and Markham divulged the incriminating activities of the Ringwoods to the county sheriff. With written, attested evidence, there was enough for Woodman to make charges.

Judge Mallard waited for Woodman on the boardwalk outside the jail. He was toeing-off the ratting cat as the sheriff stepped out, slamming the heavy door behind him.

Suggs returned the empty ration platters to the front of the jail, jumped at the bang of the door. There was half a corn pone in the skillet and he gnawed at it hungrily. There was also some lukewarm hominy still in the pot, and he ate that with the dishing-spoon. After four mouthfuls he took a fragment of the pone in one hand and went to look out the window.

The weak, temporary lawman of Youngsville got curious. He shuffled sideways, listened furtively, as the Las Cruces sheriff ran his shoulder close against the outside of the jailhouse window.

'That's about it,' Giles Woodman snapped. 'I guess the thread's breaking.'

Mallard smiled discreetly. 'Perhaps it's true. Confession really is a luxury of the weak.'

The young sheriff hitched his black, liveried gunbelt. 'In their cases, I would have prefered "confess and be hanged".' For a few seconds he looked thoughtful. 'On that raid at S River, I'm not certain whether we'll get a conviction for the older Ringwood. But there's four or five other counts between them.'

'What are you certain of?' Mallard asked.

'With your guidance, Judge, I think we can start with attempted theft, then build to perverting the course of justice and unlawful killing.'

Mallard nodded. 'With my guidance we'll get a lot more than that, and we'll call it murder.'

'Yes sir. The trial will have to be held in Las Cruces, or Roswell even. That's because of your . . .'

Mallard interrupted. 'I know, Sheriff. Because of my "personal involvement". I could hardly try Tadge Hamming for attempting to kill me.' He was watching the cat under the cracks of the boardwalk. 'Prejudice is a natural instinct, but not in the eyes of the law.'

Woodman stepped into the street, leaned against the hitching rail, looked up at the judge. 'I'll leave for Las Cruces when the Ringwoods are behind bars.' The sheriff kneeled to see the rat-catcher at work as he continued, 'I'll get rid of Suggs, get Chud Barker set up.'

'How long will that take you?' Mallard asked.

'Not sure. I may want to talk to all those who are charged. Say three, four days?' The sheriff stood up, grinning, pointing back under the boardwalk. 'Looks like one less rat for the town to worry about.'

'Good.' Mallard chuckled. 'But it's still got to elect itself a new sheriff.' The judge looked thoughtfully up and down the street. 'It's not easy in this town, but perhaps I can find somewhere buy you breakfast,' he said.

*

Suggs moved away from the jailhouse window. He had a quick glance at Hamming and Markham, both dejected, crushed at their lot. He thought of saying something, then changed his mind.

He went and sat in the front office, put his feet up on a desk, rolled a cigarette. He blew smoke at the cracked ceiling and contemplated the bleakness of his immediate future.

He'd been sitting for fifteen minutes when the door suddenly opened. A tall man in a suit that nearly matched Woodman's, confidently entered.

'My name's Barker,' the stranger said. 'I'm a deputy county sheriff, seconded from Las Cruces.' He looked disgustedly around the office, back into the jail. 'This place is a fly-blown dump.'

Suggs stared at the bright, polished star on Barker's lapel. 'So am I. Comes with the job. We ain't all of us fancy-pants law dandies,' he drawled in reply.

Barker swung up his gleaming Winchester .44. He pushed the tip of the barrel under Suggs's chin. 'There may be pay owing to you, maybe not. Either way, take your plate and spoon and get out.'

Suggs was unaccustomed to the look on Barker's face. The grey eyes looked through him, as if he didn't exist. He shivered, knew his time had run out.

Suggs slapped his hat against the walls as he climbed the stairs to Barton Ringwood's rooms at the Boulder Hotel.

The rancher had remained in town long after the expected return of Tadge Hamming. He was also waiting for news from El Paso concerning the S River herd. So far, he'd learned of the judge's escape and Hamming's arrest, and that Youngsville had been taken over by county lawmen.

He knew the weaknesses of all his hirelings, and he was in a black hostile mood when he saw Suggs standing beside his open door.

'If it's not something I want to hear, Suggs, you best ride for the border,' he roared.

The ousted sheriff sloped into the room. 'It ain't lookin' good, Mr Ringwood. You've heard about the law that's bin posted from Las Cruces. An' some a your boys are already banged up. They bin squarkin', too.'

'How do you know that?' Ringwood was banging the fist of one hand into the palm of the other.

'I heard that sheriff talkin' to Judge Mallard.' Suggs became more hesitant, unsure. 'I heard some things, Mr Ringwood, and I ain't too certain of what's goin' on round here. I ain't got a job no more, neither.'

Ringwood's eyes glazed, as the finger of impending doom touched him. 'I've come too far,' he said, distracted and quiet. 'I've got fewer men left now, Suggs. They'll close this town.' His words were sinking away, as though he was losing himself in another, deeply personal world. 'I don't know what's happened to Festus, an' I've nothin' from Tymes. If you help me now, Wallace, you'll be a long way up the peckin' order when it's over. What do you say?'

Suggs recognized his plight. 'I ain't got much of a

choice, supposin' there's somethin' left. How do I help?'

'I want you to blow out that jail. Hamming and Markham along with it.'

Judge Mallard and Giles Woodman were by the window of Ma Kettle's boarding-house. They'd finished their meal, sat smoking cigars, watching the day's business operate along the main street.

'One day they'll run a line north along the Tularosa Valley,' Mallard said. 'From Mexico to Kansas and Colorado. It'll open this country right up. I hear there's already ten thousand Chinamen working on the Southern Pacific.'

'And from what Markham and Hamming spilled, Ringwood wants to own it all,' Woodman added.

Mallard nodded. 'He'll have to get out of Yuma first. When will you arrest him?'

'Tomorrow, day after maybe. See how things pan out with Barker.'

Mallard smiled grimly. 'He should have cleared out Suggs by now. Let's go and see how he's getting on with the paperwork.'

The two men were standing opposite the jail when the first deafening explosion burst through its door and windows. The sky above the building's roof was rent with a gigantic shadow of dust and the ground shook across the street. Glass in window-panes above Mallard's head shivered and came crashing down around his feet.

In seconds, the jailhouse became an inferno of noise, flame, shuddering wood and adobe. Then the ear-splitting explosion was closely followed by another. Torrents of sparks were blasting upwards, descending slow and lazy, through clouds of smoke and dark fragments.

Woodman had already pushed the judge up close to the clapboarded store they stood in front of. He watched, overwhelmed, as a rigged team of bays reared, screamed in terror before galloping crazily down the street. The town's dog pack set up a barking, then a howling that cut through the sound of falling rubble and crack of ripping timbers.

Wallace Suggs stood back in an alley alongside Woodman and Judge Mallard. The impact of his crime showed starkly across his face, but nobody could see it. There'd been a gap under the jailhouse, rubbish-height, cat-height, two packed boxes of stump, explosive-height.

Suggs's horse was tethered well away from the street, and there was only one place for him to go. Unlike most of the others on the payroll, he hadn't let Barton Ringwood down. No sir, he was already well up in the new pecking order. He kicked the horse away from town, swung east towards the safety of Big Log ranch.

20

Together at Youngsville

'This town sure has taken a turn for the worse. Was a time when all I had to do was pull teeth or mend bones. Now I'm operating for bullets, knife wounds and shrapnel.'

Jethro Cave, the town doctor, was standing at the bedside of Giles Woodman. He was taking the sheriff's pulse, checking over two deep splinter wounds. 'You'll live, Sheriff. Those in the jail didn't, unfortunately.'

Woodman winced, bent his neck to look at his chest and shoulder. 'Yeah, doesn't look too bad. Thanks, Doc. How's Judge Mallard?'

Cave handed Woodman his vest. 'Careful. Don't go opening the wounds.'

'What's happened to the judge, Doc? What's the matter?' Woodman wanted to know.

Cave held out his hands. 'He died a short while ago. It was a heart attack. It would have been the shock. He wasn't a young man. I'm sorry.'

Woodman pulled on his vest, gritted his teeth. 'He told me this town was going to be a good place again, one of these days. I think he was wrong. It's a netherworld, and I'll be glad when I'm gone.'

The angry, upset young sheriff swung his feet to the floor of the doctor's surgery. 'Has anyone sifted through the jailhouse?'

'Yes. I've got a pocket watch and two rings. They were your colleague's. There wasn't much else, I'm afraid, by the time . . .'

'I can guess,' Woodman broke in. 'His wife can do the same. I'm not going to tell her how he died. Not the whole story, anyways.'

Once again the doctor said he was sorry, and walked disheartened from his surgery.

Sheriff Woodman looked at the lacerations in his dirty jacket, thumbed the star and swore loudly. He pulled it around his shoulders. 'Sort your own goddamn town out,' he shouted at the dust-caked window,

He stood in the street looking towards the burnt-out jailhouse, saw the charred black wood, still shiny with bucket water. He felt the eyes of passers-by, sensed the prejudice of blame. If that's the way Youngsville felt, if that's what they wanted, then it was fine by him. He would let them sort themselves out. But it wouldn't be until he'd done with Wallace Suggs and the Ringwoods. He owed Barker and Mallard that.

Giles Woodman made a temporary location in Judge Mallard's office. It was early evening, the town was unusually quiet and he sat alone. There was no one in the town he could trust, and Ringwood still had to be dealt with. He tried to formulate a plan, knowing that only the Wheats were that able, and had the disposition to help him. Before full dark, he'd sent the Las Cruces stage-driver out to S River with a message for Calum Wheat.

He spent most of the next day waiting. He asked questions, discovering just how many townsfolk were underfoot to Barton Ringwood.

At dusk the S River party rode into town and Woodman arranged a meeting in the judge's office. Sitting with Calum and Budge Gourley, he was listening to Marge Wheat.

'Yes Sheriff, it *is* my ranch, legally, that's the documented name. But my brothers know they have equal shares, always have had. Calum's got the mortgage paid up now and there's some money over. S River is going to stay ours.'

'Legally, maybe, but I don't think Ringwood's going to recognize that. He's come too far. If he weakens, the town'll see its chance. And there's blood on his hands.' Woodman responded.

'You think he's still gonna try an' take the ranch?' Calum asked.

'I do, yes. When do you expect your brother back?' The sheriff's eyes flicked from Marge to Calum.

'He should have returned with the others,' Marge said. 'But he told Budge he wanted a day in El Paso.'

'Yeah, that's right. He said he'd be watchin' our backs,' agreed Budge. 'My guess is, he'll be back tomorrow. If he heads straight for S River, Nate will send him in.'

'We'll wait for him, stay overnight, get rooms at Ma Kettle's,' suggested Calum.

Woodman nodded. 'From what I managed to pull out of Teal Markham, it seems Ringwood's got himself a hired gunman. Name of Tymes. I've also discovered some of his men have already left him. But you can bet on Wallace Suggs having joined what's left of the pack.'

Calum looked worried. 'We sent Judd Finch and his men back to Durango,' he said. 'Didn't think there'd be any need for 'em to stay around. Right now, Nate's out there on his own.'

'We know Ringwood'll stay well away,' Budge offered.

'Yeah, but his spawn won't, nor the hired gun,' Calum added.

'What happens if they ride in while we're here in town?' Marge wanted to know.

Woodman looked at her. 'Can't say, miss. All I know is, we'll need your brother from what I've heard of him. Let's hope he gets here soon.'

Ethan arrived the following morning. He was looking strong and excited. 'You going for Ringwood?' was the first thing he wanted to know. 'That family's gonna get itself blown away.'

Outside the judge's office Budge ran his hand across the roan's rump. 'What happened here?' he asked, seeing Ethan's handiwork with needle and thread.

'A nasty little story of Ringwood and his cronies.

Budge gave Ethan a surprised look. 'Festus? Where'd you cross him?'

'I didn't exactly, just his sport. They followed us down to El Paso all right, but took the main trail.'

Marge looked up and down the street. 'Where's Elky?'

Ethan climbed down from the roan. 'She drank some water along the trail. It was polluted though, real bad. Her death's another I'm putting down to the Ringwoods.'

Woodman sensed the atmosphere of pain and reprisal. 'We'd best get ready. If they're only half smart, they'll have been watching your ranch, seen Ethan leave.'

'We can make it back by noon,' Ethan was impatient, found it difficult to think of much else. 'Nate said to bring back some provisions. Grain feed an' flour,' he remembered.

'I've got all I need,' said Woodman. 'We'll load your supplies on to the stage. Me an' the young lady can ride in comfort.' He looked at Ethan and Budge. 'Budge, you look as though you can handle a stage team. Ethan, you can ride shotgun.'

'You want me inside, or on top?' Calum asked.

'I want you here in town. We don't want all the Wheats out there.'

Calum looked at the sheriff, unbelieving. 'So you're taking Marge into a gunfight?'

Marge held her hand up to Woodman, turned to her brother. 'It's legally my ranch, Calum, and we don't know there's going to be any more shooting.'

Woodman looked at Calum and shrugged. 'I kinda guessed it,' he said, half smiling.

Ethan reached out his hand, gripped his brother's arm. 'It's what I came back for, Cal, an' someone has to keep an eye on Ringwood. He's holed up somewhere. Go find him,' he insisted.

'Yeah. The Boulder Hotel,' Calum said, disappointed but accepting his task. He turned to Woodman. 'If you could have posted someone out at Big Log, Sheriff, we'd know where they all are, instead of guessin', waitin' for the bullets to fly.'

'You know of anyone hereabouts that I could've put that trust in? No. We'll just take it as we see it, and leave in an hour,' Woodman said, with the sheriff's authority.

21
Taking the Stage

As the coach splashed between the willows of S River, Budge raised his hand against the light. His eyes swept the house and outbuildings. 'Looks real quiet. Don't even see Nate around,' he said.

'We're sure makin' enough noise to rouse him,' Ethan shouted back.

Budge swung the team into the yard. The traces strained as he jammed his foot against the brake lever. They drew up between adobe sheds and a corner of the main house.

Budge leaned down, spoke into the side window of the stage. 'Stay quiet, keep outa sight,' he said. He looked towards the house. 'Nate,' he called out.

Ethan frowned. 'Looks deserted,' he said. 'He should be here.'

Ethan saw Budge's eyes drop to the sawn-off shot-gun and the Spencer carbine.

Budge looked around again. 'I don't understand. You don't think. . . ?'

Before he finished, one of the shed doors crashed open. Moving into the narrow opening, Rafer Tymes stood with a rifle pointed up at Budge and Ethan.

The gunman remained silent, calm and totally prepared. He stepped into the yard, closely followed by Wallace Suggs. The ex-sheriff of Youngsville was holding a sawn-off shotgun which he too swung up to cover Budge and Ethan.

Suggs looked agitated, doubtful of his ground, but his shotgun held steady. 'You two heave your guns over the side.'

Budge groaned, raised his revolver from its holster.

Suggs jerked the shotgun. 'Very careful, lad,' he said, grinning slightly as Budge let it drop over the front wheel.

Ethan sat unmoving, until Tymes looked at him and nodded. With his left, Ethan pulled his big Remington and tossed it after Budge's Colt.

'Whatever you're carryin' in the boot,' Suggs continued, 'drag 'em out.'

Budge muttered something under his breath. He reached down, gripped the breech of the Spencer lying next to the sawn-off shotgun. He curled his finger through the trigger-guard and lifted the big carbine.

Gritting his teeth, Ethan hissed, 'You'll get us all killed.'

Budge hesitated, then stood up. He looked into Tymes's eyes, then let the carbine clatter to the ground.

'That all you got, cowboy?'

Budge nodded. 'That's all you're gettin'.'

Tymes missed the shade of Budge's reply. 'Then get down,' he said.

Budge twisted away. He leaned to climb down, his foot stretching to the wheel below. As his right hand closed around the shotgun, he mumbled something to Ethan.

Ethan bent towards him, his back to Tymes and Suggs. 'There's probably more of 'em,' he said quietly.

Budge grunted a short reply as he swung up the shotgun. 'Then I'll die findin' out.' He leaped from the stage, away from the wheel, the scatter-gun swinging towards Tymes and Suggs.

As Budge's finger pressured the trigger, a single shot exploded the oppressive stillness. Ethan saw Budge run forward, three, four steps, lower and lower until his body rolled into the ground. Budge's outstretched arm pushed the shotgun ahead of him, his other hand clawing once at the dirt of the yard.

Through the instant grip of revulsion, Ethan looked up, swore, ugly and unbelieving at Tymes and Suggs; then beyond, to where a cloud of powder-smoke curled from a front window of the ranch house.

Ethan looked back to Budge. He wondered if the S River ramrod was just lying doggo, playing for time, but he knew different. The set of Budge's body already had the dead look. He thought of Marge. Had she already seen the killing? What was Woodman doing? The sheriff was carrying enough hardware.

Suggs's voice stung Ethan back to the moment. 'Jesus, I wasn't ready for that,' the man gasped.

Suggs then swung around as Festus Ringwood

stepped from the ranch house. 'Hit him on the run, Festus. Never knew you was that good,' he blurted out.

Festus Ringwood glanced up at Ethan, his eyes taking in the ragged blinds of the stagecoach. 'I knew he'd try something stupid,' he said. Festus was holding a Winchester, had a plated Colt tucked into the belt of his trousers.

Ethan climbed down and walked towards Budge. He turned him gently, holding his head away from the ground. He averted his eyes from Budge's chest where he knew the rifle bullet had taken him. He gripped a handful of Budge's coat and glared up at the young Ringwood. 'You've killed him, you vermin. I'll put you in Hell for this. You an' your father, both.'

Festus flicked his eyes backwards and forwards, from Budge to Ethan.

'Why'd you kill him?' Ethan's voice faltered with wrath.

Festus remained silent, but Tymes spoke up. 'He was always gonna die. He just decided to be first.'

The gunman then glanced quickly at Wallace Suggs. 'Two don't need a stage. Poke your gun inside, Suggs. Careful you don't get it chewed off.'

Kneeling next to Budge, Ethan watched Suggs open the coach door, saw him start. In the instantaneous grip of fear, Suggs took a step back. Marge came out first, her eyes fixed on Budge's lifeless body. Her body shook violently. She stepped to the ground, crumpled against the open door of the coach. Giles Woodman hesitated, then followed when Suggs thrust the shotgun at him. He unbuckled his two-gun belt, then held

Marge's elbow, supported her at the same time as stopping her falling towards Budge.

Ethan was locked into Tymes. He knew that Ringwood's hired gun wouldn't be affected by the shooting. He'd remain composed and predictable. The one to watch was Festus Ringwood.

Ethan was breathing deeply. He switched his attention to Festus, who was standing arrogant but skittish, both hands cradling his Winchester. He was waiting for the next move, and Ethan knew the danger of even blinking too fast.

Woodman's voice cut the tense atmosphere. 'You better start thinking, Tymes, and you Ringwood. I'm a county sheriff from Las Cruces. If anyone else here dies while you're holding a gun, I'll see to it personally that you hang.'

Tymes thought for a second, then spoke to Suggs. 'Take the girl inside.'

Ethan looked around him, suddenly fearful for what was going to happen. 'What's hapened to Nate?' he said.

Tymes's eyes flicked to Festus, then back to Ethan. 'Don't know who you're talkin' about.'

'Nate Starling, our top hand. Where is he?' Ethan rasped.

Festus smirked, pointed his Winchester off towards the back of the ranch house. 'He fell off that little bridge. Looked like he had a real bad headache.'

Ethan knew then they were all going to die. He watched Suggs take Marge by the arm, saw Festus looking on.

Marge looked imploringly at Ethan, but he couldn't move, daren't twitch as Suggs pulled her away from Woodman.

The sheriff tried again. 'Let the girl go. You can't win this one. If you don't let her go, you'll have to kill her. You goin' to let that happen, Tymes?'

Festus sniggered. 'He's really somethin', ain't he, Rafer?'

But Rafer Tymes was thinking. 'Old Man Ringwood can decide who lives and who dies when he gets here,' he said.

Woodman snapped at Tymes. 'If that's all you can come up with, I'll make the decision for you. I'll walk away and take the girl with me.'

Festus laughed. 'That river's gonna contain some fat fish by the end a this day Rafer.'

Woodman shook his head in disbelief. 'They'll hang you without a trial, Ringwood.'

Festus raised his Winchester, smiled hostilely at Woodman. 'Start your move,' he said, walking towards the sheriff.

Woodman glared, took a step towards the advancing Festus. Festus swung his rifle, then slammed the stock up and into the front of Woodman's face. 'Now you won't be goin' anywhere or yappin' either,' he snarled as Woodman fell at his feet.

Tymes shook his head. 'No one's leavin'. You'll all be here when Mr Ringwood arrives. He'll want to see the S River culled once an' for all.'

Ethan rose slowly to his feet. 'What you going to do with us until then?' he asked.

Tymes pointed at one of the adobe buildings. 'You'll sleep in there. Take the girl. Festus won't mind, will you, son?'

Festus's jaw was working, and Ethan could see that someone else was very close to dying.

'At least I won't have to pull a flour bag over my head,' he said. He looked at Festus and winked. 'Ain't that so, son?'

Ethan pushed the goading as close as he could, hoping that Tymes wouldn't afford the Ringwood brat any more killing. The gunman wouldn't want to risk the proof of his own work and his bounty.

'What you going to do with Gourley and Woodman?' he asked of Tymes.

Tymes looked across at Suggs who was still holding on to Marge. 'Let the girl go. Get rid of Gourley, and move this one into the house,' he said, nodding at the crumpled body of Woodman. 'Then run that team a horses into the barn.'

At the Boulder Hotel in Youngsville, Calum Wheat was suffering from a bad headache. He wasn't in a peaceable mood as he shoved the clerk up the stairs towards Barton Ringwood's rooms.

'Just say there's a message. Any more than that an' I'll kill you,' he hissed at the clerk.

'Who is it?' Ringwood asked at the tentative knock, his voice devoid of its usual authority

'It's me Mr Ringwood. I've a message for you.' The clerk was pulled away from the door by Calum.

As the door gradually opened, Calum slammed his

way into the room. Ringwood was holding a glass of bourbon, and Calum saw a small hand gun on the edge of a chair.

'Drink it,' he shouted at the rancher. 'Drink it or I'll find a way to drown you with it, slowly.'

Ringwood put the glass to his lips, saw the cold loathing in Calum's eyes, then swallowed. 'What's going on, Wheat? What do you want here?' he spluttered.

'I've come to have a final look at you, Ringwood.' Calum saw Ringwood's eyes flick to the chair, and he stared hard. 'Just try. Please just try for it,' he pleaded.

Calum shook his head, winced immediately at the pain. He pushed his own Colt back into his belt, picked up Ringwood's gun. 'You're a washed-up old man, Ringwood.'

'I ain't washed up, Wheat, and I ain't that old. Not yet.'

Calum took a step forward. 'No, not yet. But you say anything more I don't agree with, an' you'll be dead. *That's* old.'

He reached out his hand and grasped the flesh at the front of Ringwood's face. He sqeezed hard until his head hurt again, his fist shaking with tension, then he shoved the man down and away from him.

'Sit quiet, you son of a bitch, while I tell you about the next stage of your life,' he said, with a sharp, frozen edge.

Darkness fell rapidly across S River. Ethan Wheat's mind was spinning with despair and frustration. He'd spend the night with Marge, presumably under guard in one of the adobes. He knew the outbuildings well enough, hoped it was a toolshed they'd be forced to take shelter in. At least there'd be a chance to effect a get-out or to fashion a weapon of some kind.

Tymes had a look in one of the smaller adobes. He indicated that Ethan and Marge should enter. There was no door.

'A room for the night,' Tymes said. 'And if Suggs here sees as much as a shadow, we'll burn it down.'

Suggs edged forward. 'Another fire'll sure heat up the night,' he gibed.

For a short while, Ethan had a challenging look at Tymes, Suggs and Festus. He turned away in disgust, bent his head as he stepped into the dark adobe. He saw Marge huddled in a corner of the back wall.

It was a near-empty tack-shed, there were no windows, and Ethan could hardly see her in the gloom. It went through his mind that at that moment she was as likely to be as afraid of her own brother as she was of Rafer Tymes and Festus.

He hunkered down opposite, thought of saying something, then stretched his legs, sat with his back against the wall, listening for any tell-tale signs.

Within minutes, the adobe was in full dark. But in the yard Festus and Suggs were building up a fire. The yellow glow quickly shafted through the open doorway, lighting the tight, curled form of Marge.

Festus and Suggs'll stay by the fire all night, Ethan thought. He wouldn't even make it through the doorway. Suggs would shoot, and Festus would shoot to kill.

Images and words of Budge filled his mind. He wanted to walk into the dark, and kill. Shoot, strangle, knife, it didn't matter. Just extinguish Festus's life. But he couldn't, and the cancer of revenge grew inside him.

He heard Marge make a sound, and he peered across at her as she started to move along the wall towards him.

'Where's Woodman?' she asked, simply.

'He's all right,' Ethan answered.

'Yes, but where is he, Ethan?'

Ethan held up his hand. 'Keep quiet and don't come any closer, Marge. Stay where you are. If they see movement in the light, they'll fire through the doorway. Just don't move.'

Ethan rolled on to his stomach and crawled towards the door. He stayed close to the wall, until he could see through the doorway. The fire was dying down to smoke and cracking embers but just beyond it he could make out the shape of a man wrapped full-length in a blanket. He stood up slowly, hugging the rough wall, inched his head into the night. Within seconds, he heard the distinct click of a handgun being cocked. He jerked back, wondering which of the three it was.

In the intense dark of the adobe, he looked towards Marge. 'Woodman must be in the house,' he said. 'Tymes aims to keep us separated.'

'What do they want?' Marge whispered.

'They've all got their reasons, Marge. Ringwood wants everything below the Mason–Dixon line, Festus still wants you, Suggs ain't got nowhere else to go and Tymes wants his pay-off.'

Ethan sensed the bitterness in Marge's response. 'That gunman is the only one who'll likely get what he wants.'

'Yeah, that's why he's waiting for Ringwood,' he said.

22
The Last to Die

At first light Ethan edged into the doorway. In the crisp, cold air Festus and Suggs were stamping and beating their arms against their chests, but Festus caught the peripheral movement. He quickly drew his Colt, aimed it precisely at Ethan's head.

Ethan shrugged off his fatigue, disregarded the threat. He shouted out towards the ranch house. 'How long you waiting, Tymes? You really think Ringwood's comin' out here?'

Ethan waited until Tymes opened the door of the ranch house, stepped on to the veranda, before he carried on. 'You really believe he's gonna pay you off, support this pathetic, hodad sheriff? You think he cares any more about his reptile son? You believe any a that, Tymes?'

Ethan was prepared for a bullet, but it never came. Festus had caught the drift of uncertainty, the possible truth.

'He's looking after his tail. Probably half-way to Mexico by now. You'll all be left to hang or rot in the pen, whether you kill us or not.'

Ethan let his words sink in while he looked around the yard, scanned the outbuildings and barn. 'What've you done with Woodman? Where is he?' he demanded.

'Digging holes out back. We gave him a lantern. Even I know about corpus delicti.'

'What're you talkin' about?'

'No body, no crime. You and the others musta kept on ridin'. That's why you used the stage. For anyone that's interested, none of you came anywhere near the ranch.'

'You're mad, Tymes. Never had you down for that. Dull-witted maybe, but never mad.' Ethan was pressing hard again. 'You're forgettin' Budge Gourley. You think my brother's goin' to let any of you live after what's happened here? He'll hound you to Hell.'

Tymes buckled on his gunbelt, thought for a second. His eyes didn't leave Ethan, as Woodman stepped around the corner of the ranch house.

Suggs levelled his shotgun and beckoned the sheriff out front.

'I been listenin' to your friend,' Tymes said. 'You want to stay here or ride back to Las Cruces?'

Woodman looked from Ethan to Festus and Suggs, then back at Tymes. He garbled through his smashed mouth. 'I don't know what game you're playin', Tymes, but I'll stay here. This is where my work is. It's what I get paid for.'

'Wrong, Sheriff. Your work's in Las Cruces. You shoulda stayed there. Diggin' your own grave in the

Santa Rosa *ain't* what you're being paid for. I'm givin' you all the chance to live or die.'

'What chance?' Woodman slurred. He thought, then backed away a few steps. He looked at Ethan, turned and started to walk single-mindedly towards the stage.

Tymes watched him, his eyes half-closed against the rising sun. 'Not much,' he answered slowly.

As Woodman approached the empty stagecoach, Ethan realized what he was doing. The sheriff was going to get his rifle. He'd probably hidden it under the bench seat.

Festus was thumbing back the hammer of his Winchester as Ethan yelled. 'No. No, Sheriff, leave it, they're gonna kill you.'

Tymes waited until Woodman's body was framed in the doorway of the stage before he spat the words at Festus. 'Do it.'

Holding the Winchester waist-high, Festus Ringwood fired. He waited for the first bullet to find its mark, then continued, pumping, watching enraptured as the .44 bullets slammed Woodman's body into the supply sacks on the floor of the stage.

Wallace Suggs ran forward to the mangled, bloody sheriff. He looked back to Festus, then Tymes, then nodded his head.

'Get him outa there,' Tymes shouted. 'Hitch the team up and get rid of the body.'

Tymes walked threateningly to Ethan who stood overwhelmed, rigid with shock. 'If Ringwood don't turn up in an hour, youll be joinin' your friend,' the gunman rasped.

'And if he does, it'll be different? You're worse than those cowardly scum, Tymes. If Ringwood doesn't show, you'll run,' Ethan offered, quietly.

Tymes looked hard at Ethan, then heaved a tight fist into his stomach,

Ethan made the slightest smile of satisfaction as he went down, as Tymes booted him in the face.

Festus walked to the doorway of the adobe and looked inside. 'Kin a yours needs some nursin',' he said, evilly.

There was too much adrenaline rushing through Ethan for him to be badly hurt. The time was right, and it didn't take long for him to work out a plan with Marge.

Tymes had ridden to the river bends. He was reined-in beneath the willows, looking south, edgy and concerned at Ringwood's absence. Suggs was in the barn rigging out the stage team.

Exaggerating her genuine distress, Marge kneeled in the adobe's doorway. She pleaded, 'Someone help me, please.'

The 'somebody' was going to be Festus. 'What's your problem, little lady? You too need some nursin'?' he sneered, advancing towards her.

Ethan was lying in the far corner, nearside to the door, playing the dummy. He was outsretched, appeared unconscious.

Curious and eager, Festus stepped inside the adobe. He leaned his Winchester against the wall, had another look at Ethan.

As he moved further into the adobe, Ethan opened one eye, looked up through the crook of his arm. Ironically, he hoped, he willed Festus on to Marge. Keeping his eyes fixed on the back of Festus's head, Ethan carefully rolled himself on to his knees. In the thin light, he caught a glimpse of Marge's face, saw her flinch. But Festus saw it too, turned, and Ethan caught the gleam of the plated Colt as it swung around.

He sprang, his left hand reaching for the long barrel, pushing, twisting it back violently. Eighteen hours of dread and pent-up fury broke from Ethan's body. His right hand closed over the trigger guard, then he jerked down, viciously. He winced, gritted his teeth as Festus's wrist fractured. He wrenched the gun upwards, closed his eyes as the gun exploded under Festus's jaw.

Ethan went down with Festus, his face falling through a soggy crimson mist. He pulled the Colt away from Festus, stumbling backwards as he got to his feet.

He heard Marge gasp. The explosion was still booming in his head as he shouted at her. 'Don't look.' He turned to the doorway, seeking the presence of Tymes and Suggs.

Rafer Tymes had already turned his horse, was spurring back to the yard, gun in hand.

Ethan jammed Festus's Colt into his belt, grabbed the Winchester beside the doorway. 'Come on, Tymes,' he yelled. 'Let's see how good you are.'

Tymes didn't falter, he rode straight at Ethan. He kept his nerve, levelled a handgun at arm's length. Ethan was almost looking down the barrel, saw the mania of contest in Tymes's face before he fired.

Tymes fell heavily to the ground as he took the first shot. He rolled on his side, one hand gripping his stomach, but his other hand was still holding his Colt. The gunman never made a sound, just lifted the gun at Ethan.

'You're already dead, Tymes. It's all over,' Ethan rasped. He dropped the Winchester and stood with his arms at his sides. He watched Tymes, heard him curse, saw the Colt inevitably swing towards him.

Ethan stood amazed at the gunman's measure. 'You've still got to try, haven't you,' he muttered. He drew Festus's Colt from his belt and cocked the hammer. As he locked eyes with Tymes he pulled the trigger. The gunman's eyes emptied, then his big body convulsed, turned lifeless into the warm ground.

Ethan actioned the Colt again. He knew if he stepped into the open there'd be a response from Suggs. It wouldn't be head on, like Tymes. It would be from cover of the barn.

He stepped from the doorway with his back against the wall. Let Suggs have a good look at the body of Tymes. Let him wait a minute or two before Ethan took up the fight again.

Marge was standing against the far wall, her hands clenched, banging against her thighs. 'Is he still in the barn?' she asked.

'Yeah. Makin' out his last will and testament. He won't be too long for this world.'

'What will you do if he doesn't come out?' she said.

Ethan smiled. 'I'll hang a curtain across the door an'

we'll have a meeting. I'm sure we'll think of something, Sis.'

Ethan picked up Festus's Winchester and in quick succession pumped five bullets into the door of the barn. 'Suggs,' he shouted. 'Get out here before I run out of ammo.'

There was no answer.

He aimed for the leading edge of the door frame and called, again. 'Suggs, you cowardly scum, come out or I'm comin' in. Make your choice.'

He saw the door open, then the powder flash. He fired with it, levered another round and fired again, then waited in the silence.

He tossed the Winchester aside, checked the chambers of Festus's Colt, stared numbly at the shiny, nickel plating.

The sun was reaching its high, cruel point when the team of horses rattled and jinked into the yard with Suggs holding on to the off-side lead.

Ethan held the gun at his side, waiting, watching as Suggs strangely slapped the team away from him. He put a hand up against the fierce light, wondered if Suggs had a fight plan.

Ethan guessed the team of horses had done the wrong thing, gone the wrong way. Whichever, they'd left Suggs standing alone.

The man responsible for the deaths of Hamming, Markham, Deputy Chud Barker and Judge Mallard backed up against the clinkered barn. He was holding the sawn-off shotgun. He looked once at the body of Tymes, then up, as Ethan moved out of the doorway of the adobe.

'Here's where it all ends,' Ethan yelled at him.

Suggs gave a fleeting, crazed expression as he swung the shotgun, wildly loosing off both barrels.

Ethan winced at the noise, tightened his finger on the trigger. Both charges slammed into the adobe walls, either side of his body. One head height, the other somewhere near his left knee.

Suggs lurched back against the barn wall, fear stamped across his face.

'That's both barrels,' Ethan shouted. 'Reload, dead man, I'll give you time.'

He gave Suggs the time to thumb in two more cartridges, even time to snap up the barrels and take aim again. But that was all.

'It don't even things up,' he said bitterly, as he took deliberate aim and fired.

But Suggs didn't hear. He was already dead, twisting, staggering backwards, falling spread-eagled into the hard-packed soil.

Ethan let the Colt drop from his fingers, didn't look again at Suggs. He turned towards his sister, his emotions wasted.

23
The Ranch

Calum and Ethan Wheat sat their horses a mile off S River ranch. They watched a coyote lope swiftly across the deserted yard, cross the timbered strap of bridge behind the house.

'Pa built that up from nothin',' Calum said quietly.

Ethan was still watching the grey dog as it skirted the willows around the river bends. 'Yeah, I know, an' I know what you're thinkin' Cal. But it can be good again.'

Calum saw the dog swing west towards the foothills. 'This land's had too much killing over it,' he said.

'There's nowhere out here that hasn't. It's up to people like you to start over.'

'And what about you?' Calum asked.

'In me coming home, we lost everything.'

Calum pursued his thoughts. 'I asked you to come home, don't forget, and we haven't lost everything. We'll breed horses. Bring mustangs from the Pecos.

Think about it, Ethan. That roan of yours is the finest piece a horseflesh in New Mexico, and it'd be a good beginning. We could change the name of the ranch too, if you like. Call it Ethan's Hat, or the like.'

For a while, Ethan paid heed to the suggestion. Then an intimate, sad expression crossed his face. 'Supposin' I thought it was a good idea, would Marge want me around?' he wanted to know.

Calum shook his head. 'Not right at this moment, no. But she'll come around. You're still her brother.'

Ethan grimaced, for Budge's death was still wearing heavy. He stared east towards the Sangre de Christos, saw the coyote take a lingering look back. It marked its trail, then disappeared among the scrub-pine and scree of the foothills. He took a long, penetrating look at Calum.

'You never did tell me what happened to the man that started all this. He didn't even turn up for his own fight. Do you really think he fled to Mexico?'

'That's where he was headed all right. Him an' Gil Morrow.'

'You going after him?'

'No need,' Calum replied, enigmatically.

Ethan suddenly understood. He shouted, as his brother turned away, 'I reckon Barton Ringwood never even made it to the border, Cal.'

The two men rode slowly back towards the ranch house. Ethan noted its rugged, blocky shape against the flat rangeland.

'Yeah,' he said. 'My Hat. Let's give it a go.'